Author Profile

Maxine Handy was born next to a wood in Kent, and had a view of the River Thames from her bedroom window. However, she spent her formative years in a small village beneath a wood (Birchanger) on the Herts/Essex border. From there she attended school in antique Saffron Walden where she joined the choir, giving performances of works by Benjamin Britten. Lucky enough to encounter an inspirational English teacher she won many prizes before reading English Language and Literature at the University of Leeds, completing a dissertation on Henry James' short stories of the literary life for her MA. University also gave her an opportunity to study Classical Civilisation and enter the elite seductive atmosphere of the Greek Department. She is also increasingly fascinated by, and drawn to Jewish history, culture, and literature. The author now lives in a tiny village in rural Cheshire, enjoying writing, countertenors, and the company of her two beloved cats and two adult children. She visits mainland Greece and Italy at every opportunity. Having published *The Life of Bosworth – A Cat* in 2007, described by Julian Clary as 'A charming and surprising read', Maxine is now working on the novelisation of a countertenor memoir, to be published next year.

Also by Maxine Handy

The Life of Bosworth
A Cat

Published by Maniot Books 2007

The Wishing Well and Other Fantasies

Maxine Handy

British Library Cataloguing in Publication Data
A catalogue record for this book is available from the British
Library

ISBN 978-1-4461-7622-1

To

Dr Robert Oliver Chapman MB ChB

'Good books tell the truth, even when they're about things that never have been and never will be. They're truthful in a different way.'

Stanislaw Lem, in conversation

The Wishing Well and Other Fantasies

Contents

The Wishing Well

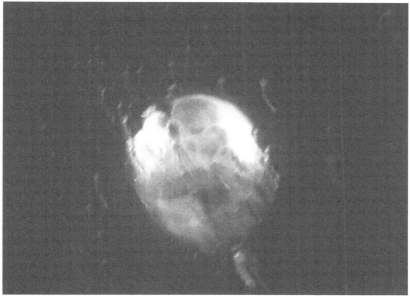

Reflection in well

Tímas, aged 13, and her younger brother Ilias, aged eight, were young Greeks from the austere Mani: the middle finger of the southern Peloponnese. In the spring of 2008 they had abruptly moved with their parents to the island of Sardinia, the second-largest island in the Mediterranean but nonetheless an isolated, primitive and faraway land.

Before arriving in their chosen village of Sennariolo, near Bosa, a tiny rural community in the north-west of the island, the bookish and intellectually-precocious Tímas had read extensively on the subject of her new home. She had begun her quest with D H Lawrence's strange travelogue *Sea and Sardinia* written in 1921, which described the landscape as 'savage, dark-bushed, sky-exposed', beset by a primordial silence disturbed only by the wind. Tímas thrilled to this description, and learned that during his travels with his German wife, Frieda, Lawrence had visited the then impenetrable Gennargentu Massif, the highest peaks in the mountainous area of Barbagia. Tímas read that this central eastern part of Sardinia was, for centuries, the domain of shepherds who lived there with their large flocks in almost complete isolation. These nomadic shepherds were often in conflict with the more settled crop farmers, living in the foothills of the mountains, and bloodthirsty feuds ensued. Sometimes entire families were wiped out in revenge attacks or sheep rustling. This *Warrior Shepherd* society with tribal values was similar to that of the Mani, her own homeland in southern Greece. And like the beloved Taygetos Mountains which formed the mythological backdrop to her Maniot village of Kardamyli, the distant peaks of the Gennargentu were often dusted with snow, even in early May.

However, it was reading about the single most dominant feature of Sardinia's landscape, the ancient, prehistoric *Nuraghe* which enthralled and enchanted Tímas and Ilias. Seven thousand or so of these strange, conical, stone fortresses were dotted about the island. Some extended into grand settlements that predated the arrival of the Romans, by more than one thousand years. Dating from approximately 1800 to 400BC these truncated conical structures were made out of huge basalt blocks taken from extinct volcanoes. It is thought that the towers were used for shelter and for guarding the surrounding territory. The name *nuraghe* derives from the Sardinian word *nurra*, which means 'heap' or 'mound'. Tímas was accustomed to this uncertainty and confusion; her own origins in the Mani were linked to a possible meaning of the word *Maniot* as 'insane'.

The young Greek girl was eager to know more about the human beings who had inhabited these formidable dwellings, but it seemed that very little was known about the Nuraghic people. Judging by their buildings, they were well organised and had remarkable engineering skills, but they appear to have left no written word. Tímas' book contained startling photographs of Nuraghic artefacts. The *bronzetti* (statuettes) observed the historians, suggested a tribal, highly-stratified society of aristocrats, priests, warriors, artisans, shepherds and farmers.

Whilst looking at the captivating photographs of the dark, rather brutal-looking *nuraghe*, Tímas came across a picture of a place that would change her life forever. The image depicted a sacred well temple, mesmerising in its simple geometry. From as early as 1800BC, people had started raising *nuraghe*, and from about 1100BC the inhabitants of Sardinia began to construct elaborate *pozzi*, *sacri*, or sacred well temples, in association with their defensive stone towers. Three thousand years ago, the nuraghi peoples worshipped the waters.

Tímas found an extensive description in a chapter titled 'Mystery Towers, Fairy Houses, and Sacred Wells'. The author explained that the *sacri* discovered today display many common traits. This includes a keyhole-shaped opening in the ground, with a triangular stairwell leading down to a well. The wells always face the sun and are so orientated that during solstice the sun shines directly down the stairs. Thus the sun's rays 'descend' the staircase at the entrance to the well, eventually reaching the sheet of water.

However, a still more enchanting phenomenon is repeated every *18 years and 6 months*, and is known as *the moon in the well*. It occurs when the moon is at its maximum declination and is entirely reflected in the sacred water. This rare event represented the most important and enigmatic element of Nuraghic rites. As the sun represents fatherhood and fire, so the moon symbolises motherhood, enchantment, and the feminine sign of water, 'I feel ... I protect ... I treasure loved ones and my home'

Amazingly, *the moon in the well* was due to appear that very summer, their first in Sardinia! This was fate, drawing them to the Santa Cristina well in Paulilatino, amidst the ancient olive groves. The proximity of trees, associated with wisdom, made the water especially effective at healing diseases of the eye. Tímas was reminded of the violent and poetic obsession with seeing and the eyes in Shakespeare's *King Lear*.

The building techniques for wells were more refined than those employed in the *nuraghe*, and 'nowhere is this more evident than in the Santa Cristina site, north-east of Oristano. The lines of this well temple are so perfect that it looks like it was made yesterday. Thirteen basalt steps make a precisely-carved descent to the spring.'

Tímas and Ilias knew that this fascinating and beautiful place was quite close to their new home. Their father had always encouraged them to become confident riders, and allowed them a pony. Amos, their 10-year-old grey gelding, had come with them to Sardinia; they would ride him to Santa Cristina! Flushed with excitement Tímas whispered to Ilias that they would soon be jumping into the beautiful old saddle, and riding off to a unique adventure. She promised that they would journey all day and take a lovely picnic, including walnuts, fruit and honey cake.

Ilias only lost interest when the book moved on from ancient history, and described the cycle of invasions, conquest, and defiance which had given Sardinia its rich and complex culture. Phoenicians, Carthaginians, and finally Romans, had all landed on the large island, followed by the Pisans and Genoese, who were later supplanted by the Spanish. In 1479 Sardinia became a Spanish territory, but in 1714 the north-Italian Savoy Kingdom took possession of the island, until after Italian unity in 1861, when Sardinia once again fell under the control of Rome. The beautiful low-lying areas of the coast interspersed by lagoons, like those of the Sinis peninsula, remained largely unpopulated until the elimination of malaria in the 1950s.

Ilias felt restless after taking in all this information, and wandered off to play with, and feed, all his animals. He left his sister dreaming of a magic well. To Tímas the sacred wells of the *nuraghe* indicated the existence of a water cult such as she was familiar with in Greece. At school, Tímas had been taught that the Greek gods were forces of nature, as exemplified in the relationship between Poseidon and the sea, and thus of science. In Homeric heroic religion, although the gods have existence outside the material world, they are thought to express themselves directly in natural events. 'The fundamental assumption that there is a pervasive underlying substance out of which everything emerges and into which everything returns is attributed to Thales of Miletos. Thales was apparently led to this conclusion out of the belief that the world was full of gods, and his unifying substance, water, was similarly charged with spiritual presence.' Tímas had read this extract in *The Non-Local Universe – The New Physics and Matters of the Mind*, by Robert Nadeau and Menas Kafatos.

In the nuraghic sanctuary of Santa Cristina, Tímas had discovered her fairytale *Pan's Labyrinth*, an interface between the natural and supernatural which might provide a solution to her present crisis. She longed to experience non-sequentiale time, and to find her Telion. Events are determined not by cause, but by purpose. Tímas longed for *Perfectos*.

Her father had brought his family to Sardinia to live in the province of Oristano. She had now discovered that the prehistoric complex of Santa Cristina, under a canopy of ancient olive trees, was situated in Oristano and easily accessible. This pagan power of the underground shrine would enable her to discover the whereabouts of her newly-vanished father. It was to be a journey with her brother Ilias – a journey of luminous shade, towards beauty and difficulty: Heaven and Hell, perhaps.

Even before her father had disappeared into the vast mountain range, Tímas had felt close to the spiritual world.

Because Nuraghic civilisation remained shrouded in mystery and myth, but was undoubtedly centred on water as a sacred portal, it connected to Greek thinking on an opening or bridge to eternity. In ancient Greek mythology, the sun god, who came from Heaven providing light for the day, was believed to disappear into the sea at night. Water was seen as a vital and precious resource for the dual nature of man: body and spirit. Wells were places where the positive power of light could enter and spring out of the earth water, giving the opportunity to reach eternal life.

Trees growing by water, as in the olive grove at Santa Christina, were associated with wisdom, and those waters especially effective at healing diseases of the eye. To have the full effect on curing the malady, the person drinking the water had to sleep immediately. This idea was fundamental to the Greek cult of Asclepius at Epidauros. Seeing a play was part of the therapy involving healing of the mind through dreams and visions, whilst sleeping. During sleep, or on first waking, the patient would have received prophetic visions or dreams. The healing power of the waters was due to the hydrological spirit who lived in them; this linked to the severed head idea of the Orpheus myth. Many of the thirty or more nuraghic wells in Sardinia have a connection with the severed head. As the soul was thought to reside in the head, the ultimate power force, the head being detached from the body was seen as the final act of sacrifice. By placing the head in water, it might be possible to repossess the mind of the deceased as it flowed forth into the water.

Tímas wanted to question the dead, but she decided to use her father's divining rods and keep the spirits at a distance. Her father had explained to her that the ancient practice of water divining uses the ability of animals to discover a watering hole. This ability indicates their closeness to, and dependency on, the earth. Tímas felt as one with the animals; she was at her happiest when living in their kingdom. On three occasions during the last six months, she had been disturbed at night by Athena's owl, and then fully woken by a voice speaking intimately to her. She called it *The Voice in the Night*. It was always the same male, resonant baritone voice, seemingly positioned beside her right ear. At first, Tímas was very distinctly aware of his cool gentle breath against her warm ear. This sensation awakened her completely, and she no longer felt alone in her bedroom. The man's powerful voice then said only one word, but the single word had changed on each occasion.

On the first visit it was 'don't', then some few months later 'think', and then recently 'love'. The voice was very beautiful; it startled but never frightened Tímas. She sensed that she was being visited by someone who wished to impart a very special message but one which seemed deliberately enigmatic and ambiguous. When hearing the single word and the intensified breath, resembling a cool evening breeze on a warm flowery shore, she was fully awake and receptive solely to the voice. Somehow it was beckoning her, but having given the solitary message, the voice immediately withdrew and the overwhelming presence disappeared. There was no gradual fading, just an abrupt departure of the disembodied voice.

For a few moments Tímas would concentrate intently, trying to understand. But at the moment she felt close to understanding the purpose of this intense encounter, the clarity of the voice was obscured by swirling, dizzying memories, which dissolved as she again fell into a profound sleep. The strange, ecstatic visitation, albeit so brief, seemed to control her waking and sleeping thoughts, but *she* was never able to speak to or question him:

Was he giving her a message?
Was he imparting a memory?
Was he telling her about the future?

Perhaps she was being told to go on her intended journey 'beyond the uttermost stars'.

The Narrative of Tímas

My father is mysteriously absent in the mountains of the desolate Gennargentu Massif. Since arriving in Sardinia in the early Spring I've been reading about the island, to help me understand why my father brought us here, why he has disappeared and where and how I might locate him. There are so many questions. The sacred well at Santa Cristina is the key. I know it is.

When in Greece, my father used to go off alone and walk in the Taygetos mountains, with just his dogs and our pony, Amos, a grey gelding. My brother and I were not unwanted or abandoned by our father. He simply said that he wanted to live with the shepherds, and find the wolves which once roamed the mountains in great numbers. Legend says that these wolves still exist, and that sometimes shepherds are killed by them, their bones found months later scattered near the limestone mule paths, known as Kalderími. But I think these terrifying wolves are mythical; nowadays they have probably been hunted to extinction. Father used to entertain us with stories about the folk legends of the Peloponnese, especially ones about animals, and about sitting in the cypress groves at midday – in order to see the ghosts of this ancient landscape. These eerie visions come at midday in the brilliant sunshine. They just appear at the haunted hour, moving towards you like some dark light, but remaining just out of reach. Many people say that they have seen Achilles with the shade of Patroclus standing beside him. I rather like this idea of a private pantheon of the dead. In our dreams we often meet our deceased loved ones and have conversations with them, so why should we be afraid of meeting (seeing) them when we are awake? Although, I must admit that after reading Henry

James' *The Turn of the Screw* I decided that daytime ghosts are the most frightening of phantoms.

Ilias and I loved these tales of the supernatural, but my mother believed that if allowed too much wild freedom in this mythological atmosphere, where *time* stands still, we might become feral children like the twin boys Romulus and Remus. She reminded us that although in ancient days Romulus had founded Rome, at one time the greatest city in the western world, he had also slain his brother Remus. She felt the ancient history of Greece and Italy encouraged tribalism and dissent between different groups of people. My mother did not share father's love of classical civilisation. She was a devout member of the Greek Orthodox church, but believed that the family should move to a 'modern' country like Australia or Canada, where we might become rich and could forget out burdensome history and the ambiguous legacy of antiquity.

But one day in the early spring of 2008 my father decided to leave his country of birth and move to Italy in search of an earthly paradise. Unlike his wife, he was not interested in material possessions. Unlike my mother, he was attracted to the primitive and the pagan, and decided to search for them in impoverished mainland southern Italy.

However, after much reading and thinking, he decided to go instead to the mountains of northern Sardinia. There he would seek work and travel within the shepherd communities. He loved the idea that the forebears of these same people had been the island's first inhabitants. The nuraghic people had been led by warrior-king shepherds, and until the two recent decades they had continued to live in *Pinettas*, huge cone-shaped huts of stone and juniper wood. Furthermore, these shepherds still tended their large creamy-white flocks in remote areas, but nowadays they usually returned to their villages at night. It is true that one of the most beautiful things in Sardinia is watching the mass of luminous sheep with musical tinkling bells moving slowly together at dusk against the darkening-green of the hillside. The whole vision seems eternal.

But, ultimately, it was not my father to whom the ancient days revealed themselves. It was to me, Tímas and my little brother Ilias.

My small brother and I arrived in the tiny village of Sennariolo in April 2008. The very first day of the following month marked the beginning of summer. It also marked the onset of our beautiful but terrifying adventure in the prehistoric settlements of the Sinis Peninsula.

Whilst our father disappeared into the bare windswept heights of the Barbagia region, and mother withdrew to the bare stone courtyard of her cool, white shuttered stone house, my brother and I found our new friends in the eerie, blue-grey light and wild flower glazed meadows of thousand-year-old olive groves.

Then, during one particular summer twilight at the end of May, whilst playing hide and seek outside the walls of a nuraghe, we met our first spirit child. The antique olive grove in which we played was carpeted with asphodel, the immortal flower of paradise and Elysium. And the profuse white daisies recalled the Basilica of Santa Maria della Neve, (St Mary of the Snow), to which my father had taken us on first arriving in Sardinia. The dramatic pealing bells of this great church rang out over the plains below, and transported us to heaven.

The spirit child beckoned to me, and holding my brother's hand we followed our guide. The ghostly, birdlike presence moved inside the walls and further towards the inner sanctum of the deserted nuraghic village, stopping to beckon us forward when we seemed to be gliding away. My brother and I were enchanted, as though we were under a spell, but the magic was tempered by fear. Eventually, having drawn us in towards the centre of the grove, the spirit child stood still by a narrow-walled flight of perfectly-smooth, stone steps, which led downwards to an underground miraculous spring. Having brought us to this place of veneration, the spirit vanished.

My brother and I did not understand the meaning of this strange visitation and sudden departure, but I decided to discuss it with another of our new friends, a local shepherd named Giovanni Dore. He played the traditional Sardinian pipes, had three large dogs and rode a donkey called Ariadne.

I had first consulted the shepherd within a few days of my father's disappearance. Giovanni explained to me that many people had gone missing, or been lost forever in the Gennargentu. It was a treacherous and unforgiving place, a hostile environment which should be treated with great respect.

Giovanni dismissed stories of man-eating wolves, but told us about fierce wild boar and giant predators, which he said were demons of the ancient forests. But most importantly our shepherd friend told us about the magic power of the sacred well. In olden times, he said, these powers had been used to solve problems and submit people to the justice system by anointing their eyes with the sacred water. If guilty, then they would be blinded but if they could see, then they were proved innocent. The keyhole stairs leading down to the well were like a passage to the underworld where the water level rose and fell. The nearby stone oculus enabled one to look down into the well far below, and see a perfect reflection of one's face, framed in the circle of the water below. It was a geometric and mystical experience, like looking through a telescope into a mirror.

A few days before my conversation with Giovanni, I'd taken a photograph of my brother, Ilias. When I looked at the digital image I noticed a bright orb by Ilias' back. It was a clearly-defined disc which seemed to me to be an emanation from a spirit being. I knew that an eminent experimental physicist, Klaus Heinemann had been doing research on these 'orbs', and concluded that they are a manifestation of the paranormal. Klaus Heinemann believes that analysing and understanding these 'orbs' has implications for the way we view our world and physical death. Appearing in our photographs is an attempt by the dead to communicate with the living, and most astonishingly, says the physicist, 'if you "ask" the orbs to appear, they show up more often in your photos, especially at happy gatherings'. The presence of the shining orb in my photograph seemed to me to prove the existence of the spirit world, and that consciousness survives physical death, but it also appeared to confirm the tragic fate of my father.

Now that I believed my father must be dead, I longed to look into the underworld. I told Giovanni about our encounter with the spirit child who had shown us the sanctuary of Santa Cristina. The shepherd said that we must use the mysterious and magical powers of the water in the sacred well to divine the truth; he added that the spirit child (or phantom bird) was a sign for us. We must enjoy and persevere with conversation.

Giovanni believed that the world of the living and the world of the dead were equally interesting and intersected at special places like the nuraghic wells. The mind of the shepherd combined the pagan and the Christian, and as a Greek I was very familiar with this metamorphosis. My own brother, Ilias, was named for the highest peak in the Taygetos, Profitas Ilias which means the prophet Elijah but also refers back to Helios, the Greek sun god. On the peak is the church of the prophet Elija, and many people hike to the summit on the evening of July 19th, to participate in a service at sunrise, honouring the saint's name day on July 20th, but also honouring the sun. In perfect weather conditions the peak of the mountain casts a perfect triangular shadow at sunrise, said to remind us that this was the temporary hiding place of Christ after the resurrection, before he ascended to his father in heaven.

Giovanni said that all I needed to pass into the afterlife was, not a blood sacrifice like the ancient Greeks, but copper divining rods. Through these my communication with father would become ever more intricate and change my perceptions forever. I would discover parallel universes. He said that fate had removed my father so that I could learn 'the secrets of one who had passed over'. This process would be both ecstatic and agonising, tender and cruel. My olive grove would resemble the Garden of Gethsemane, and although I would remain human and mortal, I would connect with the invisible divine close by, just above me in fact, said Giovanni, adding that it would be as depicted in mediaeval paintings.

In going down through the dark but luminous well, I would rise into the suspended ecstasy of the life beyond. The shepherd promised that I would learn from one who was himself learning to adjust to his new place in the Universe. Through my simple metal rods I would glimpse eternity. And perhaps my beloved father could tell me where to find his body so that I might wrap it in the antique Sardinian funeral textiles, *tapinos de mortos*.

Because I was seemingly bereaved, I remained wary of the effects of grief. I had seen, and been deeply affected by, Nicholas Roeg's film *Don't Look Now*, described as 'The greatest film every made about grief and the supernatural'. The shock of losing my father might make me vulnerable to a seemingly supernatural presence. On the other hand, I also knew about the work of Professor Michael Heller, a polish priest and mathematician, a pioneering cosmologist and philosopher specialising in mathematics and metaphysics. Professor Heller argues against the Newtonian concept of creation, that is, against the idea of an absolute space and an absolute time, and of God creating energy and matter at certain times. He suggests that modern theologians should go back to the traditional doctrine that the creation of the Universe was an act that occurred outside space and time.

In pursuit of Homer's world of heroes, warriors and myths, my father had walked the mighty Taygetos Mountains of the southern Peloponnese. The Taygetos are *the* mythical mountains. According to Greek mythology the range was named after the nymph Taygeti, one of the Seven Pleiades and daughter of Atlas. She fled the unwanted attentions of Zeus by turning into a hind, but only after she had given birth, by Zeus, to a son, Lakedaimon 'the lake demon'. Taygeti hanged herself, but her son became the local hero and gave her name to the tremendous mountain upon which she had hanged herself. Lakedaimonas was the ancestor of the Spartans with their blue eyes and flowing blonde hair. Ancient Greeks believed that the goddess Artemis, patron of hunting, and her golden-horned deer, lived in Taygetos' ravines and on her peaks.

Father had even followed in the footsteps of Neoptolemus, the renowned son of 'godlike Achilles' the swift-footed son of Peleus. When the time came for Neoptolemus to claim his bride he was given the task of crossing the Taygetos Mountains; he had to walk all the way from old Kardamyli to Sparta, following the ancient Kalderími (mule paths) through the mountains.

Kardamyli is still a small village made of harmonious stone houses, set in lush green surroundings. In spring it is wonderful to smell the flowering shrubs and aromatic bushes, including heavenly thyme. From the Taygetos you circle down to the village like an eagle. Kardamyli is also famous for being mentioned in the Mycenaean period of Homer's *Iliad*. King Agamemnon tried to mitigate the wrath of Achilles by offering to him the 'city' of Kardamyli, along with several other cities; and under the Romans, the emperor Augustus offered Kardamyli to Sparta so that it could have a port of its very own.

My father was a proud Maniot from the feudal, fortified Mani, the only area of Greece never occupied by the Turks. During the Turkish occupation of Greece, Taygetos with its castle-houses, hermitages and monasteries, became a safe-refuge for the Greeks. Ilias and I loved to walk with our father; a favourite excursion took us on the path up from old Kardamyli to Agios Sophia Church. On the steep climb we passed the fortified tower complex of the old village, and then followed the mule path as it ascended through cypresses and olive groves. Father would tell us about the war hero and writer Patrick Leigh Fermor, whose books had made the Mani famous, and who lived in a beautiful secluded house, surrounded by cypress trees, in our own village of Kardamyli. Patrick, known as 'Paddy' was a friend of the famous explorer Bruce Chatwin. When Bruce died 'Paddy' accompanied his ashes to the Byzantine chapel of Agios Nikolaos in the village of Chora just east of Kardamyli. They are buried in an unmarked grave beneath an olive tree in front of the beautiful church. For my brother and I, the highlight of the walk to Agios Sophia was passing the empty graves of the Dioscuri. These were Mycenaean tombs carved in the rock, which seemed to glow at twilight as though they were lit from within by the moon. The Dioscuri were the twins Castor and Polydeuces, offspring of Leda and Zeus. In works of art, the boys are depicted in flowing white gowns with stars in attendance around their heads. They became the protective gods of sailors and hospitality; when they died Zeus turned them into the constellation Gemini. The Dioscuri have always remained special deities for the Lacedaimonians. Stars and heavenly motifs are a popular outer Mani motif on lintels and doorways – a tribute to the benevolence of the Dioscuri. Further on from the tomb we used to search for the fossilised snakes, an amazing sight on the ancient Kalderimi, trodden by so many of our shepherd and warrior ancestors.

Not surprisingly, given his heritage, when my father moved to Sardinia and visited the Barbagia, he again identified with the outsiders. The original Barbagians ('barbarians') had fled from Roman rule and found refuge within a highly-traditional but defiant society. Like the people of Barbagia, Father resented state-imposed authority. He was sick of conformity and government control, and for him, nothing expressed this rebellion better than the famous Sardinian murals.

When we visited the Barbagian village of Mamoiada, south of Nuoro, with its extraordinary sinister mural of the *issohadores* and *mamuthones* – representing, respectively hunters and hunted - I knew that this depiction of a terrifying pagan festival had affected him deeply, and quickly drawn him into the desolate mountains of the Gennargentu.

In the mountainous regions of Barbagia carnival celebrations are attended by wild characters wearing ferocious masks in the guise of animals and devils, and acting out dramatic pitched battles in village streets. Like Orgosolo, known as 'the bandit capital of the Island', the poor and run-down village of Mamolida is famous for its warrior shepherds in violent conflict with the settled crop-farmers on the Barbagia's fringes. This tension, along with rivalry between clans, often found expression in sheep-rustling and murder, but also in the carnival ritual procession. The *mamuthones* (the hunted) are clad in shaggy sheepskin jerkins, their faces covered in chilling, heavy oversized black wooden masks. Their dark sheepskins are hidden beneath rows of jangling sheep-bells with which they create a discordant clamour. Meanwhile, the 'hunters', the red jacketed *issohadores* attempt to lasso their quarry, including bystanders who are supposed to appease them with gifts of wine and sweets. As the two columns of spooky masked *Manuthones* advance solemnly along the main street (Corso Vittorio Emanuele), they perform curious synchronized leaps, causing the hundreds of sheep-bells tied across their backs to clang simultaneously, while the *Issohadores* twirl their lassos and ensnare their victims, often from a distance of several metres.

My father adored the rebellious spirit of this region with its political message of exploitation, and the many oppressed by the few. His love of freedom and escape meant that conformity tormented him, driving him ever higher towards emptiness and the infinite.

I felt afraid for him in the Gennargentu as our shepherd friend had told me that every year many 'tourists' disappear on these disorientating tracks, and even experienced hikers vanish, never to be seen again. The many wild animals add to the sense of danger, although I knew that Sardinia is the only part of Italy that does not have venomous adders, or, for that matter, any kind of poisonous snake. 'But,' repeated Giovanni, 'Walkers often mistake sheep tracks for proper paths, and become irrecoverably lost.'

Anyway, the haunting mural of 'hunters and hunted' took father's mind captive as surely as the very lasso depicted in the wall painting. Fed up and at odds with the feminisation of society, this mural was the essence of masculinity, courage, danger, and physical strength. For the same reason, father loved horse-riding. His favourite mount was a fiery chestnut stallion named Rustum, and he knew that the Sardinians are the most renowned equestrians in Italy.

Shortly after seeing the Mamoida mural, our father bought some traditional carved wooden animal masks and put them on. One in particular was particularly menacing. It resembled a goat and was jet black in hue, with long curling horns like those of a mouflon. In Sardinia these masks are prized and respected; they are reserved solely for special festivals and carnivals. The village people, like Giovanni, are very superstitious and still believe in witchcraft. I was afraid that my father would be seen trying on his mask collection and thus invite revenge attacks upon us, or alienate us from the local people whom I wished to come to know. Father had given my brother Ilias some traditional musical instruments, including reed pipes and a dog-skin drum which has a terrifying sound. It is reputed to have been used by shepherds to ward off evil spirits, and is of nuraghic origin. This strident instrument is cleverly made of cork and formed by a base covered in a membrane of dog-skin with a string fixed in the middle of it. Up to the beginning of the nineteenth century this peculiar and menacing instrument was also used by brigands to unsaddle gendarmes.

I had heard the sinister sound of the 'su trimparu' when my brother and I watched the Sardinian film *Padre Padrone*, about a small boy enslaved as a shepherd by his tyrannical father and sent out to the mountains to live with and guard the sheep. The fear and isolation of the lonely, abused boy had touched me deeply and also affected my brother Ilias. Every time Ilias played his drum, the small shepherd boy and harsh landscape of the bleak film would come before my eyes.

However, my father worshipped this patriarchial society and often listened to recordings of Sardinian shepherds' songs, which reflected these values he so admired. His favourite group was the traditional polyphonic quartet, *Tenores di Bitti*; they come from the small mountain village of Bitti, and the origins of their singing date back to the era of *nuraghes*. This precious cultural heritage is handed down orally from father to son, and the words of the songs reflect everyday life in the agricultural world. The themes include love and religion, but the Tenores' singing is characterised by the sounds of the natural landscape – sheep bleating, cows bellowing, the wind hissing. The singers stand one in front of the other, forming a circle – a symbol of male strength and cohesion. Their roots are deeply established in the ancient culture of Barbagia – 'There exists a true magnetism and solar energy between the granite land of Sardinia and the Tenores' singing'. Many of their records were made in the countryside *nuraghe* and include the ambient noises of these locations. One of my father's favourite songs was *Lamentu*, a mourning song of an innocent young man, arrested in Bitti and sentenced to 24 years in prison for a murder he did not commit.

My mother never spoke of father's mysterious absence; she refused to look in that direction. But Giovanni told me that darkness led to light. I must have courage and enter the well. He explained that this ancient water source was in the 'domus de janas', meaning territories rich in traces of the past which are considered by tradition to be the ideal sites for witches, and for black and white magic. In conclusion, Giovanni confided that several nights ago he had heard the sound of 'su carru de sos mortos' – the ox cart of the dead, whose squeaking is said to be heard when somebody is dying.

With Giovanni's words lingering in my ears, I once again clutched the hand of my brother Ilias, and entered the imposing remains of the nuraghic settlement of Santa Cristina. To distract myself from the purpose of our visit and its conclusion in the well, I called to mind the guidebook facts about the complex: 'A wide-ranging site scattered among a shady grove of olive trees, comprising a *nuraghe*, a sacred well, and long house. The site dates back to 1800BC but has been added to by the Carthaginians and Romans. The nuraghe's main tower, about 15m high, has a *tholos*-type interior, into which niches and alcoves have been hewn. The shrine of the sacred well is reached down a narrow-walled flight of perfectly smooth steps. The site is most impressive – enhanced by its mossy green ambience.'

As I descended into the well, my head was spinning and I could hear the rapid drumbeats of my heart. To steady myself I again recited words of description from the many sources I had unearthed: 'In the midst of an olive grove, the sacred well and other monuments from the nuraghic era exude a powerfully pagan atmosphere'. Instead of comforting me, these words heightened my sense of foreboding of thousands of ghosts from both the ancient and recent past, pressing down upon me. Ilias' hand in mine was moist and slippery as we descended the steps. Were we about to experience events blocked from ordinary perception?

As Greeks, metaphysical or psychic phenomena were familiar to us. In Ancient Greece the mortal and divine existed in close contact; the Greeks are at their ease with the idea of transitional planes of existence, marked by sacred, sometimes marginal, places like the many remote sites which have an entrance to the underworld. We all know and love the story of Orpheus descending in search of his Eurydice. It is easy for a Greek to pass 'serenely from reality to dream'.

The well water at the base of the steps had an obsidian blackness as dark as the black volcanic stone found in Sardinia and known as 'Neolithic black gold'. When we had reached the last step and were on the very threshold of the water, I looked into the well and saw the reflection of our father. It occurred to me even at the very moment of apparent contact that the well might be acting as a mirror reflecting my own brain and its memories, including those which my father had communicated to me in the past. He had told me the story of his first youthful love affair with a girl who had subsequently died by her own hand. He had outgrown the once passionate relationship but she had never recovered from the loss of her beloved. I wondered if this image of my father was simply a manifestation of my own vulnerability to a powerful and tragic sense of loss. If it was true that my father's mortal life had ended, it was also true that my love for him would live on.

My feelings of heroism in overcoming fear at this moment were tempered by memories of my adopted uncle, Piers, and his wife Ruth. It was Piers who had first introduced me to the use of divining rods. Recently bereaved, he was mourning the sudden death of his beautiful wife. Within a few weeks of her burial he was convinced that he was in almost daily contact with her via his divining rods. He wrote down and analysed all his conversations with her as though conducting a scientific experiment. Although she never visited him in human form she returned to him as an otherworldly invisible presence. At night she shared his bed; he could sense her outline and feel her breath on him. According to my bereaved uncle, they even enjoyed a post-mortem sexual relationship. He refused to give details of this private event. Piers was deeply religious; he believed that a divine being was facilitating this miraculous contact between the living and the dead. My father knew that Piers had frequently been unfaithful to his wife, whereas she had truly loved him with absolute fidelity and devotion. He had not loved her as she had loved him. So perhaps this avowed communication with Ruth was a means of seeking redemption and forgiveness for his guilty betrayal of her perfect love. Piers had convinced himself of God's intervention in their tragedy. My father felt that Piers was gripped by a dangerous and obstructive obsession in seeking encounters with this phantom.

My brother and I turned to look back at our descent through the keyhole; our downward flight into nothingness. As we gazed upwards, an indistinct shape seemed to move slowly towards us, blurred by the sfumato of the olive grove. My thoughts fled to the Hindu belief that with its last breath a spirit returns to the place it loves the best, there to remain for one day and night … Had my father come in search of his children? Was his severed head lying beneath the waters of the well?

The indistinct outline came closer; it changed into a shimmering, thin, vague stain, before finally transforming into the familiar presence of my father. His eyes, as blue as lapis, looked into mine as he drew us to him, lifting me up and holding me close. Tenderly he folded us both in his arms, pressing his face against mine.

Had he returned from the land of the dead? Or never been there at all? Or, like Odysseus, had he been on a long journey without ever forgetting home and always longing to return there. A safe haven, perhaps? Perhaps we had both been confronted by the natural and the supernatural, the one having metamorphosed into the other. With what had I been communicating in the sacred well? I let go of the thin copper rods and allowed them to disappear into the water. The tiny ripples soon vanished and once again the opaque surface was mirror still.

As we began our upward flight and walked together in the atmospheric twilight, leaving behind the magic well in the ancient blue-grey olive grove, I knew that our departure was forever. As we trod gently on the damp grass I thought of the words of the countertenor James Bowman, on singing Elizabeth Lutyens' *The Tears of Night*: 'I like the sort of Chiaroscuro feeling, of one moving from darkness into light all the time through a sort of twilight.'

We would go back to Greece and never return to the haunted beauty of this territory.

Ilias' Story

My sister Tímas has told you our story and everything you need to know about is contained within her narrative. But she did forget to mention the cats. I found them wandering in the musty olive grove at St Cristina. They were thin, hungry and neglected so I took them home to love and care for them as family pets. I named them Kambos and Taygeti, Maniot names ready for our journey home to Greece and the beautiful cypresses of the Peloponnesus in Kardamyli:

'One evening just at sunset we laid him in the grave;
Although a humble animal his heart was true and brave.
All the family joined us, in solemn march and slow,
From the garden place beneath the trees and,
Where the sunflowers grow.'

Blue Zoisite for Lovers

Villa Rufolo

Preface

The great myths are founded on a combination of triumph and tragedy. Consider the godlike hero Achilles, swift-footed son of Peleus, fatally flawed by his vulnerable heel: the only part of him that was not dipped in myths river. Or imagine the Louvre's Nike of Samothrace as it stood long ago in the cabeiric sanctuary of the Great Gods. This ancient statue embodies victory and mourning. A friend told me recently that these were precisely the dual emotions she felt on visiting Gettysburg and remembering the words of Abraham Lincoln's address, delivered there on the afternoon of Thursday November 19th, 1863. His speech took place at the dedication of the Soldier's National Cemetery, four and a half months after the great and decisive battle in which the Union armies defeated those of the Confederacy. More than 7,500 soldiers had died and 5,000 horses. Lincoln arrived on horseback for the event; his saddle that day is still extant. The speech was brief but America still stands in its symbolic shadow. There are clear parallels between Lincoln's elegy at Gettysburg, and Pericles' Funeral Oration during the Peloponnesian War as described by Thucydides, although Lincoln's rhetoric was inspired by the King James Bible. The imagery used is that of birth, life and death, and it is as much an exhortation as a lament. Lincoln reminded his audience that there was unfinished work to be done; the living must bring to fruition the achievements of those who had fought in battle. He merged the afterlife, the present, and the future. Lincoln's speech had the dream touch of the foreteller; he had spoken prophetically as one in a mist who might head on deeper yet into the mist.

Now imagine a contemporary story of two young adults on their world travels; an adventurous journey towards matrimony. Full of danger and ecstasy: Africa in particular baffled and beckoned. Their arrival in Tanzania was a response to an irresistible call.

Blue Zoisite for Lovers

The day had come at last. After months of planning, waiting, and longing, it was the morning of her departure for East Africa. Thomasina had chosen Tanzania as the appropriate destination with which to conclude her journey around the world. In early childhood she had listened to her granddad's stories of his time there during the Second World War, and many years later had been given his photographs of Nairobi where he lived in a colonial bungalow. Her dark-skinned, green-eyed, grandfather gazed out from the tiny monochrome picture; a monkey was seated on his shoulder and a large cat lazed on the verandah. Grandad had always loved animals and cared for any strays that came his way. He explained to Thomasina about the beauty and danger of Africa; death could come quickly. Out in the bush it was necessary to be accompanied by a native guide; the Africans noticed danger signals long before the Europeans. Poisonous snakes, like the deadly Mamba, could appear from nowhere and strike suddenly. Hippo, crocodiles and buffalo were fascinating when viewed from afar, but a fatal encounter could develop if humans came too close. Rhino were not aggressive, he said, unless they had young to protect. Their appearance in full charge was alarming because of their size and bulk, but really they were mostly harmless. Lions were fine as long as they were not injured or hungry; it was man who had invaded *their* territory. When on excursions in the bush with his African guide, granddad said that he always had a fire burning close to his tent. In those beautiful moonlit nights he loved to listen to the roaring of lions, hyenas cackling, and the earth-shaking trumpeting of elephants. Each morning when he climbed out from beneath his mosquito net he found a friendly chameleon inside his tent, most welcome as it preyed on insects. Grandad made sure that he protected his feet from 'jiggers', and always examined his army boots for scorpions.

However, Thomasina's favourite photograph, still treasured, was of her grandfather standing in the vast African grasslands with a snow-capped Mount Kilimanjaro in the background. This was the image which had inspired her to follow in his footsteps. Long after the war had ended, granddad still spoke frequently of the amazing African moon and the awe-inspiring grace of the giraffe moving across the plains, as though in slow-motion.

Thomasina's grandfather had died when she was only ten; his ashes were buried underneath a memorial stone in her local churchyard. A few years later she kept her pony, Amarilli, in livery at the adjacent farm. As she rode in the paddock or indoor school she used to wonder if granddad could watch her from the afterlife.

By the time Thomasina became a young adult, her addiction to travel was firmly rooted. Beginning in Europe and North America, she soon embraced most of the planet. After completing her first degree and before continuing with post-graduate study, she decided that a volunteer work placement in Tanzania beckoned. Many people were baffled by her desire, warning her that Africa was full of pitfalls for the unwary. Unless one travelled in luxury as a pampered tourist, it was likely that one would succumb to horrific diseases. Even with preventative Western medicines, Malaria was frequently fatal. Without an air-ambulance service in place there were just too many ways to arrive very suddenly at the end of life. And with 60 percent of Africans infected by HIV what was the point of teaching them English?

No dissenting voices or tales of risk and disaster affected Thomasina's resolve. She was going to East Africa; nothing would stop her. She listened only to her inmost self; she followed her heart. What else was there for anyone but that single impulse?

So, at the age of 23, Thomasina sent all her friends and family an email from Perth, Australia. It was Easter time and she and her partner Domenico were staying with friends of his family, after spending time in the Blue Mountains. 'They have a blue air hanging over them which is caused by the oil in the thousands of surrounding Eucalyptus trees,' Thomasina informed her enthralled readers. 'Hope everyone is well and got lots of Easter eggs! I fly to Africa on Saturday and can't wait!'

Within a few days it was clear that however thrilling the first encounter with Africa, squalid living conditions quickly took their toll on the health of the *mzungu*. Thomasina's message on 23rd May 2006 spoke of their arrival in Nairobi 'otherwise known as Nai-robbery … a crazy and diverse city', with chaotic streets full of people trying to sell things. Taking a private chauffeur-driven car to visit the sights, they went to an elephant orphanage where they were able to stroke and play with the baby elephants, and also visited the house where Karen Blixen used to live; it was beautifully set in lush orchards in the richest part of Nairobi. During this rather colonial tour they saw their first baboons and a wild white rhino, just 30 metres away.

From sinister, violent Nairobi, utterly changed since Grandad's wartime years, they took a hot, overcrowded shuttle bus to Arusha in Tanzania. The dirt track drive over the baking plains was obviously amazing, passing through many tiny villages where the houses were made of mud or plastic sheets and sticks, brooded over by the great snow-capped Mount Kilimanjaro in the background which came into view just at sunset. Thomasina's photograph of her granddad from the 1940s had at last come to life. But the highlight of the journey was neither the magnificent landscape nor the wild animals; it was the numerous 'Maasai tribes we saw just wandering with their cattle over the plains miles from anywhere. They looked beautiful in their brightly-coloured traditional costumes and beads complete with spears and knives. I had to pinch myself to believe they were real and not just there for us to look at.'

Having arrived in Arusha they attended a barbecue where they met other volunteers and were entertained by the Maasai who performed some of their tribal dances, including the one where they jump up and down! 'The spectacle of 20 Maasai warriors springing relentlessly up and down whilst humming and singing in unison was fantastic.' The town was typical of Africa in its poverty, hustle and bustle and friendliness. After all this excitement it was time to sleep, in preparation for the journey to remote Pangani, where their teaching placement would commence. In the months to come, the Maasai tribes and their myths would play a seminal role in the destiny of Thomasina and her lover, Domenico.

The squalor which they immediately encountered in their Pangani accommodation was such a shock to Thomasina, that she wanted to leave at once. Thomasina was already exhausted by the heat in boneshaker buses, crowded with people and animals in the aisles, and days travelling. Nothing in the Mondo Challenge description had prepared her for the horror of their 'home'. The house belonged to Mr Saleem and was considered to be one of the best houses in Pangani because it had electricity, at least some of the time! The daily power cuts, crumbling walls and corrugated iron roofs all gave the sense of living in a hovel. Thomasina and Domenico's room was filthy and full of junk, with a bed so small that they could barely squeeze into it. Worst of all was the sanitation which was utterly revolting: 'When I was shown the "bathroom" my stomach turned – a stinky, putrid hole in the floor with no shower or running water. We must wash from a bucket and collect our water from the well. The night we arrived there was a power cut and as we lay in the pitch black we heard rats scuffling around our room. I was adamant that we were leaving but now I am used to the place.' An email from Domenico also describes their primitive environment and its effect on his beloved: '– rats in the house, scorpions and spiders in the bathroom, food cooked on outdoor fire – a hovel all in all but not so bad under the mozzie net and the families and their children are very endearing.' Being exceptionally strong and fit, and a longtime member of the OTC, Domenico was unfazed by heat, danger, or physical hardship, but tiny Thomasina, his companion, was a delicate, sensitive soul. The teaching work was exhausting in such heat, children in the morning and adult classes in the afternoon. Mzungu volunteers were held in high esteem by the local population and were treated with respect and affection; 'the locals saying "Ay up" as an English greeting!' Another frequent exclamation was 'Ay say', obviously an imitation of the quintessentially English 'I say'.

The diet was utterly monotonous but very healthy '– rice and fish, rice and fish, rice and fish'. Also, the abundance of inexpensive, delicious fruit was wonderful; Thomasina loved the small flavourful bananas, just as granddad had done. Initially, she was off school with a flu-like chest infection, probably brought on, said Domenico, 'by the sight of spiders, rats, daily slaughter of animals and me eating goats testicles'.

However, Thomasina soon adjusted and adapted, becoming used to all things African. The tropical beach nearby and sand islands two hours' sailing away, good for snorkelling and fishing, were compensations. Also, contact with the outside world became more infrequent as the nearest computer was a two-hour bus journey from their village. Once the stress subsided and her health recovered, Thomasina began to enjoy daily life in Pangani and also look forward to a two-week holiday in Zanzibar, to take place at the end of the first teaching placement.

One bonus was the lovely family living next door to them in the tiny dusty courtyard surrounded by low-lying, run-down buildings. Mary and Daniel had three children, Kasea (9), Edina (11) and adorable 10-month-old Samueli as well as their three-year-old nephew Freddy, who was living with them. Thomasina and Domenico loved playing with the children, although their noisiness at all hours was sometimes very trying. 'Eleven pm was way past the kids' bedtime in my opinion,' wrote Thomasina in her travel diary.

Opposite their ramshackle living quarters was Mama Zanana's house, which she shared with her 7-year-old niece Adijha, and her own younger sister Kay. There was also a lodger called Grace who worked as a nurse at Pangani hospital. Mama's husband, Mr Saleem, was only there very infrequently as he was busy skitting between his three wives. Thomasina and Domenico became very fond of the stereotypical African 'Mama'. She was normally to be found squatting over the coal fire in her outdoor kitchen, sweeping the yard, carrying huge buckets of water balanced on her head or barking orders at Adijha or Kay. 'She is an imposing sight dressed in her brightly-coloured Kanga and headscarf and weighs around 17 stone.'

On the opposite side of Pangani River was a lovely beach. Walking there took in the sights of secluded mud hut houses, boys playing in mangrove trees and canoes hollowed out from tree trunks, and collabus monkeys everywhere. The local representative of the charity for which Thomasina and her partner were working, was named Iddi. He was a usually-comic, ever-present character of 38 years, but he looked like a child. His broken English was neurotic and his manner over excitable. For a supposedly-educated man his superstitious beliefs were quite unbelievable; he completely believed in witch doctors and magic. He told Thomasina and Domenico a story about a woman whose husband didn't love her anymore so she went to see the witch doctor for help. The witch doctor gave her some powder to put in his food, which was supposed to make him fall back in love with her forever. Apparently, after eating the meal, the man turned into a snake with a man's head. When Thomasina and Domenico laughed at this story, Iddi became quite offended and swore that it was true. At the time it had made front-page news in all the newspapers in Dar es Salaam!

The nursery school where Domenico and Thomasina were teaching catered for 25 three to six-year-old African children. Lessons began at 8.30am and finished at 11.30am. Gombero School was set amidst farmers' fields and was about a half-hour walk away from Mama Zanana's house. The only teaching aids in the green, corrugated, iron shack were blackboards and benches, but the adorable enthusiastic children made it all seem worthwhile. Every morning without fail, 25 children raced towards Thomasina and Domenico, before they had even reached the school gates, chanting 'teacher, teacher'. Once they reached the volunteers they would throw themselves at them, before fighting one another over who was able to hold the hands of Domenico and Thomasina. The young children would hang from their fingers and cling onto their arms and legs.

The first half hour of school was spent in singing; their rendition of *Baa Baa Black Sheep* was deafening. The children worked so hard that their veins literally burst out from the necks. If Thomasina asked a question, all hands would go up and all voices shouted 'Teacher, mimi mimi (me, me)', even though most of the children did not know the answer. Also, the children were easily pleased; they were happy to play with Thomasina's hair, pull the 'strange' hairs on Domenico's legs, and sing to themselves or their dolls made from sticks. The morning lessons comprised a hard one-hour slog of repeatedly singing the alphabet, counting, or naming the parts of natural objects, such as flowers. This was followed by free play and storytime, when eager eyes and ears engulfed their feet. All the children loved storytime, and to finish the morning they played outdoor games for half an hour, exhausting in the sunshine and heat of between 30–35 degrees daily.

Thomasina never got used to the disgusting and abysmal outside toilets, described as 'stinking to high heaven on a hot day and infested with huge millipedes'. The insanitary conditions and low-lying situation of Pangani contributed to frequent cases of malaria; many were fatal.

The poverty in Pangani, a run-down backward coastal town, could be very depressing for the volunteers. Many of the children wore filthy school uniforms, wet from urine. Various ailments such as ear infections, coughs and lesions on the legs were ignored by the children's parents and African teachers, two local women named Mary and Makashi. Thomasina and Domenico were responsible for all the teaching, whilst the African staff translated and kept the discipline. Their readiness to use corporal punishment deeply shocked the volunteers, but the children seemed impervious to this threat, often jumping onto the desks and running around screaming.

The two-hour afternoon adult classes were much more tranquil. Small numbers meant that Thomasina and her partner were able to get to know their pupils very well, especially as most already had a reasonable knowledge of spoken English. Pastor Frank was a softly-spoken devout Christian, very sweet and a true gentleman. Joseph was a gruff subsistence farmer who described himself as 'a peasant'. The dwarf-like James, aged 30, was a dairy farmer, somewhat miserable and impolite at times, but his wife and unborn child had recently died so Thomasina felt great compassion for him. Mr Temba the headmaster, and also a pastor, was a delightful fellow but his progress in English was hampered by a terrible stammer. Thomasina and Domenico also taught Mr Wilson, a pleasant librarian from town, and Edward a young electrician who began all his English sentences with 'ya' and a boyish chuckle! One of their worrying students was Clara, a timid and extremely quiet woman who turned up with a black eye. The volunteer teachers suspected that she suffered violent abuse at home.

Their teaching companion Makashi, very studious and quiet, was their only Muslim pupil although Pangani itself was 50 percent Muslim and 50 percent Christian. Some of the Muslim villagers had warned others of their faith not to attend English classes as they believed that the volunteers would attempt to convert them. Despite being the friendliest of places with no overt trouble, a sector of really extremist Islamists had caused a riot only weeks before. Armed police had to come to the scene; the Muslim aggressors were trying to impose their beliefs on the rest of the community and force them to convert. The local extremist mosque, situation just behind Mama Zanana's house was known as 'the Al-Quaeda mosque' owned by a local man who had recently been arrested in connection with that terrorist organisation. Antipathy to Christians was fuelled by poverty and illness. The main businesses were farming and coconut plantations, but many people remained unemployed. Such tough lives made people indifferent to contracting AIDS and according to hospital statistics 60% of the population of Pangani were HIV-positive. In addition to sexually transmitted diseases, the often weakened immune systems were attacked by cholera, tuberculosis, and malaria, which were endemic. Thomasina and Domenico had also seen many people with elephantitus. Resignation to terrible diseases and frequent death was compounded by ignorance and superstition. The volunteer teachers were held in high regard and treated with the greatest respect and kindness. Although lovely to be placed on a pedestal, these attitudes, rooted in the past, had a negative effect on African progress. Some of the opinions were quite unbelievable. Several people told Thomasina and Domenic that 'mzungus' (white Europeans) were thought to be something very special; in the Swahili dictionary the word also means 'something amazing'. In general, said Mr Wilson of their pupils, Africans believe that white people have superior intelligence and know the answers to everything.

The local people were constantly asking questions of the white volunteers, such as what was wrong with their sick child, or wife, and also many mechanical questions about how things work. They were also curious about why people behaved in a certain way; although these matters were usually ascribed to the effects of magic or the intervention of spirits. Christianity and African superstition melded happily. However, when a white person did not know the answer to a question, the Africans were surprised and disappointed.

The Pangadeco bar seemed to be the centre of social life for many of the richer people in Pangani. Thomasina adopted a ginger-and-white Tom kitten that she named Simba, and fed him every night with leftover scraps of fish from the Pangadeco. The setting was idyllic, the bar being located amidst shady trees and overlooking the beach, but bedevilled by the ubiquitous mosquitos. Also, 'each and every day,' wrote Thomasina in her diary, 'a poor unfortunate goat is dragged off to meet its maker right in front of all the guests – I am disgusted by the spectacle, while the locals are completely unfazed.'

Whilst Domenico took his early morning run with fellow volunteer, Adam, risking meetings with wild animals, Thomasina enjoyed hanging around the house to play with the neighbour's children and the 10-month-old Samueli, who took his first steps in front of her.

Another village friend was the Rastafarian, Mashaka, whose one and only priority in life was his dope smoking routine, reported thus in Thomasina's travel journal: 'Maybe one joint before breakfast, three joints after lunch, then sleep for a couple of hours, then about 6 joints in the evening …' – that was about the extent of his conversation in broken English. Another 'chilled out' local friend was Usman, with whom it was almost impossible to communicate through language. His verbal offerings were limited to 'Domenico, Thomasina, where?' and 'OK, later'. In spite of this he was a frequent visitor and would spend hours looking at Thomasina's camera or Domenico's watch. He also persuaded Domenico to play for the Pangani football team; they were the only players with shoes, apart from the one man who wore just one trainer. When Thomasina asked him why he was wearing a single trainer, he looked at her as though she was stupid and replied 'because I have only one'.

Weekend excursions often included their untrustworthy companion Iddi; he was supposedly employed by Mondo Challenge to assist the volunteers. In reality he often just 'tagged along' and his lack of logic often drove Thomasina and Domenico to anger and despair. A visit to Saadani National Park turned to nightmare when 20 African mechanics kept swapping the tyres of their hired pick-up truck, in order to get it ready for the journey along the extremely bumpy and dusty road to Saadani village. Two hours into the drive, the vehicle got stuck in a big pool of muddy water and was extricated with the greatest difficulty. Iddy then got everyone completely lost and dusk was falling before they reached the village. However, the difficult journey had afforded one amazing glimpse of African wildlife. Shortly after at last getting their vehicle on the right track, a giraffe had crossed directly in front of the car, the first big wild animal that Domenico and Thomasina had seen. 'The way it ran was like slow motion; we were both stunned,' wrote Thomasina as she remembered the moment. Her granddad had spoken to her of just such an experience when he was being driven through the African bush in the 1940s. The beautiful, graceful giraffe had soon become his favourite animal, and looked completely different, he said, from those seen in zoos back home in England. And like granddad, Thomasina and her partner camped by the sea, marvelling at the huge, bright full-moon and the millions of twinkling stars in the night sky.

The villagers of Saadani told the young English couple that lions often came to kill their goats, but on this occasion they saw only zebra, wildebeest, gazelle, giraffe and waterhog. The animals seemed abundant but Thomasina and Domenico were disappointed that they had not seen any lions or elephants. Over the next weeks, however, they were to enjoy many thrilling and close encounters with the great predators of Africa. They would be stalked by leopards, almost make the fatal mistake of swimming with a black mamba and see the king of the beasts in all his glory.

Returning to Pangani they witnessed the appalling male African attitude to women. As a 'msungu', Thomasina was placed on a pedestal and she wrote of her superior status in the eyes of the men: 'I really do get treated as something special. The men are always so polite and courteous, pulling out my chair for me, carrying my bag, making sure I have the comfort seat in the truck etc.' This superior status as a white woman was later to prove critical in saving her life. When admitted to a terrible squalid hospital because she was seriously ill with the lethal strain of malaria, the doctor gave up his bed to her and administered his only effective tablets, because she was a 'msungu'. Of course she had taken her own medical kit for blood tests, but there was only a single supply of anti-malarial tablets available and these she was given. Her recovery was uncertain: in fact the disease had such a grip on her small body that she was not expected to survive. Lying delirious on a bed, in her own vomit and surrounded by the excrement and other bodily fluids of the dying, her partner Domenico slept on the floor beside her bed and cared for her as well as he could. It was fortunate that he was so fit and strong as he had to carry her outside to the filthy cesspit; one of the effects of malaria is constant opening of the bowels.

Thomasina later reflected on all this and how grateful she was to be alive. Her thoughts returned to a poor elderly lady she had met on the return truck journey to Pangani. The woman needed a lift to the next village 20km away because her daughter was sick. The old woman herself could barely walk, but none of the African men even thought of helping her. Domenico lifted her into the truck, and because the vehicle had been stuck in the mud and all the men had had to push the truck out, Thomasina was at the wheel. So once the elderly female passenger was safely seated, Thomasina drove her to the village so that she could tend her sick daughter. Thomasina commented on this incident in her diary: 'This is something that we have really noticed in Africa – that the women do all the hard labour such as collecting and chopping the firewood, and if they are struggling with something, the men never help them'. Needless to say, Domenico was a source of delight and amazement to the African women. He carried their children, played with them, fetched water and firewood for the women, and even helped to dig the grave of a former student who had finally succumbed to AIDS. Despite the HIV infection rate of 60 percent, and the obvious ravages of the disease, the African attitude was one of denial. It was never admitted that a relative had died from this disease, such was the stigma. It was said that the white man had brought this deadly illness, but because of his godlike intelligence he had also brought many good things. There were so many terrible diseases in Africa and horrible ways to die, in addition to poverty and hunger, that people seemed resigned to the consequences of an AIDS epidemic. When Thomasina visited a nearby orphanage where the children received only one meal a day, and had hardly any toys or educational materials, she saw at first hand the devastating effects of AIDS. This was the reality for most people in the third world; people without access to drug help but also coming from a culture which treated women so badly.

Thomasina's granddad had been incensed by the attitudes of African men towards women. Like Domenico, he had always regarding the opposite sex as equal but accorded them an even higher status and respect. The African women in the colonial 1940s had adored granddad as their helper, support and chivalrous friend in the daily struggles of their lives and all they endured.

Just as her granddad had always said, the Africans had much to teach the white people who visited their amazing and beautiful country. Domenico and Thomasina were to learn many interesting things from teaching adult classes and travelling to remote places with their local friends. The Africans were always eager to learn about life in England. They thought that the English were surrounded by wild animals like those in Africa and that if you wanted a sheep, for instance, then you could just kill and eat it! They did not understand the concept of farmers owning animals on behalf of others who subsequently ate them. Neither did they grasp the idea that someone else was paid to slaughter the animals. Most unbelievable to them though, was the practice of plastic surgery. 'At first they didn't believe us, then they were completely amazed and couldn't understand why such a thing existed. It was quite refreshing to see a new opinion as it has almost become normal in the west.'

A year later, Thomasina and her partner met up with Olengunin, a Maasai who came briefly to England wearing his chuka and sandals. He loved the greenness of England, but found it far too cold for him. During an excursion to Hampton Court, he lay down on his stomach to smell the grass, saying that he wished he could take it home for his cattle in Africa. But he was puzzled by the absence of wild animals; where were the rhino, lions, elephants and buffalo? He walked barefoot or wore only sandals; he was unused to sleeping in a bed and hated the food on offer. Whilst in England he lived on baked beans! When he had climbed the active volcano Ol-Doinio-Lengae, as guide to Domenico, he had worn only his traditional chuka and rubber flip-flops made from old car tyres. Olengunin had amazing navigational abilities and a perfect sense of time, without any need for a watch. He also noticed everything, like animal prints and imminent danger from predators. Occasionally a Maasai would be eaten by a sick or starving lion, but mostly the big cats avoided them, seeming to have an ancestral/genetic knowledge that these former warriors were fearless, brave and dangerous to them. Olengunin carried only his spear, but could almost scent danger from buffalo, hippo and leopards. Unlike the white man, he always noticed what was around him, especially in his path or advancing to his rear. It was so easy to be snatched by a stealthy leopard or two. Animals and small children were particularly vulnerable and great care was taken in the construction of Maasai Bhomas and also when sleeping overnight out on the grasslands. Layers of thorn bushes were always constructed around the people and fires lit to warn off animals. The nomadic Maasai existed mostly on meat from their domestic animals, and especially milk and blood from their precious cattle. The young men of the tribe endured a type of progress into full manhood, similar to the aboriginal 'walkabout'. Domenico and Thomasina, unusually, were invited to an initiation and circumcision ceremony which involved eating raw meat and drinking blood and milk mixed together. Thomasina ducked out in fear of parasites and food poisoning. She recognised the honour being bestowed upon her, but knew that the Maasai regularly cleansed their digestive systems by eating plants which they kept secret. They had even developed a method of immunizing themselves against malaria, which had some efficacy. Thomasina knew that her immune system would not be as robust as that of her Maasai friends; she had already exposed herself to near-fatal risks.

Olengunin's culture shock when he visited England was mirrored by Thomasina's when she encountered the Hadzabe tribe; the last hunter gatherers left in East Africa. They approached the tribe very cautiously, even after carefully negotiated 'access'. The Hadzabe men and boys are superb bowmen; their hunting is done using arrows. Adult males wear animal skin around their loins and also sometimes as a short cloak. The women use their hands to dig for grubs, roots and a type of potato which they consume raw and covered in earth. These people speak a strange language called 'click'; they communicate using a wide variety of clicking sounds and body gestures. Thomasina and Domenico went hunting with the men, which they found an amazing experience. Thomasina said it felt like returning to the stone age especially as the Hadzabe were devoid of facial expressions except for those of hostility or aggression.

After the ascent of Ol-Doinio-Lengae, the ultra-fit and strong Domenico found climbing Kilimanjaro a 'doddle'. He was amused by the struggle and 'alpenstocks' of others, and quickly reached the summit. Whilst her partner was engaged in climbing Africa's highest mountain, Thomasina was staying on a 'gorgeous colonial farm on the slopes of Kilimanjaro and doing some horseriding out in the African bush'.

When Thomasina and Domenico finally returned to England, they both pursued postgraduate degrees at the University of Sheffield. Their longing and nostalgia for all things African found expression in their choice of rented accommodation in leafy Netheredge. The landlord was Nigerian, with a passion for fine art. He had come to England in the 1970s to study engineering, and had never returned to his large high achieving family of doctors and lawyers. Hassan had been forced to study a scientific subject but his heart was in collecting art. He had married an English woman with whom he had two children, but they later divorced and since that time he had lived alone in his dark, dank basement flat surrounded by hundreds of paintings. He enjoyed the occasional company of his student lodgers, and devoted the rest of his time to attending auctions.

Despite his love for England and contempt for Africa, he retained many fascinating beliefs and superstitions form his early years. He was certain that one day the spirits of the dead would come for Tony Blair the war criminal, and take their revenge. Hassan also had some very unusual ideas about gender roles, saying that he only cooked using the hotplates, because 'oven is for woman'. When he was taken to hospital suffering from suspected pneumonia and underwent blood tests, he complained angrily to medical staff that he had 'never been with bad women'. He was convinced that they were giving him an AIDS test! His defensiveness was understandable as when he had first arrived in Sheffield there were signs on rented accommodation saying 'no blacks'. Strangely, though he was always making derogatory remarks about Africans, especially his tenants, saying that they were typically 'lazy, dishonest and disrespectful'. And when he took his regular late night walk, which he loved, he would lament that it might make women nervous to see a black man walking behind them in the dark.

Hassan never spent any money on repairs or improvements; he saw no need. Infuriatingly, hazards ranged form an unusable gas fire, to an external wooden and wobbly staircase to the top flat. When Thomasina and Domenico tried to address these dangers he would simply say 'Alee-ass-ey', as he did after almost every sentence. But they were very fond of him and on one occasion when they had nearly split up after one of their infamous arguments, it was Hassan who had persuaded them to stay together and work things through. Also, an evening visit to his subterranean flat to view his latest painting and take tea with him, was a delightful experience.

When their circumstances changed and Thomasina had to move, Hassan gave her some unusual presents with an African theme. Her new luxury flat had every safety precaution and device, but unfortunately it included a totally unsafe flatmate called Gregory. He looked like a woodchopper or mad axeman form Grimm's fairytales. In fact he was a misogynistic sexual predator form Poland, who only admired Germans. He horrified Thomasina by cleaning the kitchen work surfaces with a toilet sponge and having the central heating on high at all times, including at night.

He ate his meals at an individual table-for-one, facing the blank wall with his back to Thomasina. He hated her two cats, and when arguing showed his rotten front tooth which Thomasina could not help staring at in revulsion. Eventually, his behaviour took a very disturbing turn and he was expelled from the flat. He had placed several threatening and obscene illustrated notes in Thomasina's underwear. She had discovered them in taking her laundry to the washing machine. Informed of this the landlord evicted him immediately.

Thomasina's next flat was even worse, situated in a bleak, treeless, depressing area of Sheffield. Run by a rogue landlord, it was painted in black and red with a water feature in the back yard which looked like Dracula's tomb! The leaking roof added to the icebox atmosphere and sense of decay befitting a vampire's residence. Also, the dishwasher had an aroma of rotting flesh! When Thomasina later visited Hassan and he took her through his secret passageway into her former very comfortable flat, she felt homesick.

After all their travel and adventures, it was sometimes difficult to settle into impoverished and intense study at Sheffield. Thomasina's course was very demanding academically and involved several work placements, but she managed to enjoy outdoor activities at the weekend. She loved the City of Sheffield, where her brother was also at University, and was fortunate to live in the leafy area of Nether Edge with an African landlord. This helped to soften the blow of leaving Tanzania, which she had come to love. A place of extremes.

Thomasina intended to resume her world travel once she had completed her second degree and training in Mental Health. India was next on her list. For Thomasina, travel represented freedom, a kind of freedom which she had seen expressed in the magic wood of *A Midsummer Night's Dream*, and on Catherine and Heathcliff's Penistone Crag. As a small child, Thomasina had been a precocious reader, and literature remained very important to her. She had also been deeply affected in childhood by the extraordinary experience of twice seeing James Bowman as Oberon, in Benjamin Britten's Opera version of *The Dream*. Another profound influence and great love was the 1939 film version of *Wuthering Heights*, starring Laurence Olivier and Merle Oberon. Thomasina's mother had been a devotee of Olivier, having seen him at the Old Vic on numerous occasions. She still treasured two letters which she had received from him during his glory years in the Waterloo Road. Also Thomasina's mother had enjoyed a decade of close communication with James Bowman, the greatest countertenor in the world, having commissioned a marvellous *scena* to celebrate his 50th birthday. It had been very exciting for Thomasina to accompany her mother to recitals; James would always single her out to sing to, making his music personal and beautiful. She had never forgotten his Oberon at Sadler's Wells, especially as he described the King of Shadows as his *alter ego*. Thomasina was fascinated by the transformation of James' marvellously low and sultry speaking voice into his singing voice at countertenor pitch. It was a remarkable and bewitching metamorphosis. He described his bass-baritone speaking voice as being like a cavern in which his alto voice could resonate. This concept had been brilliantly realised by Thomasina's mother when she had visualised James Bowman as Leonardo da Vinci's *The Virgin of the Rock*. James had agreed with her entirely; that beautiful Old Master, fading with time to become an ever more beautiful masterpiece collated and immortalized his genius. Thomasina's mother had been venerated as a lustrous pearl in James' chiaroscuro; their empathy was deeply touching. For the past 10 years, Thomasina's mother had been writing a memoir *Burning in Blueness: The Dark-light of a Countertenor*. Having at last finished the piece, she gave copies to both Thomasina and her younger brother, Jolyon, saying: 'My soul craves the dark-light so I listen again to a countertenor lost to me for a decade'.

Thomasina had long identified with wildness, turbulence, and non-conformity. Her proper place was in Oberon's anarchic wood with Titania's luscious sensuous bower, or Heathcliff and Catherine's Penistone Crag. Just as her mother, in May 1972, had fallen in love with the Britten/Purcell realisation *Sweeter Than Roses*, a song of seduction performed by James Bowman and Benjamin Britten, so the heart of Thomasina yearned for a dark-soul.

World travel would transport Domenico and Thomasina to thrilling and unforgettable destinations, but two places remained especially precious - the 'cool evening breeze on a warm flowery shore' in Positano, and the Brontë landscape of heather and butterflies in Domenico's home county of Yorkshire. The two had shared many holidays in Italy, where

Thomasina was always thought to be Italian, and walking together on the moors around Haworth. After almost 10 years of knowing her, and having finally completed his officer training in the RAF, Domenico decided to 'crack on'; the time had come to propose marriage to his beloved. He would be triumphant. He had always wanted children; he and his wife would be fruitful and multiply.

Domenico knew how much Thomasina loved *Wuthering Heights*, so this was his chosen place to offer lifelong love. It was a highly romantic but turbulent location, ideally suited to their devoted but stormy relationship. Not only had Domenico found a sublime, elevated situation on which to offer himself forever, but concealed inside his trouser pocket he carried the perfect gem, redolent with meaning. This day would be inspired by Heathcliff and Catherine, the actual wedding by their having fallen truly in love on the Amalfi coast, and the later English reception by *A Midsummer Night's Dream*. Moonlight and madness on June 26th 2010, but today – TANZANITE.

The most coveted colour for this unique gemstone is a blue surrounded by a delicate hint of purple; one of the most extravagant and magical colours known to man. 'An exceptional tanzanite will continue to fascinate with its unusual, captivating aura', wrote the New York jewellery company Tiffany, a short time after the discovery of this gemstone. These qualities made it the only choice for Thomasina's engagement ring, now to be carried up to Wuthering Heights.

For a long time, these precious crystals were hidden from the eye of Man. Formed on a vast plain in the shadow of Kilimanjaro, they are found nowhere else in the world. Stories of their discovery are varied, some entering the realm of myth and the mystical. One straightforward version says that passing Maasai simply noticed sparkling objects on the ground and went to investigate. But at the time of tanzanite's discovery, local Maasai tribesmen wove bold and colourful stories around the creation of this exceptional stone, drawing on the rich folklore and legends of their beautiful country. They told that the land was set ablaze by a bolt of lightning and that the heat from this magic 'fire from the sky' transformed crystals on the ground into shimmering blue-violet gems. When the last cinders dissolved into the earth and the thick smoke settled, awestruck tribesmen filled their pouches with the mystical stones intuitively knowing that these jewels would bring a better life.

However, the origins of tanzanite remain shrouded in mystery; the most widely accredited version is the story of Ali Juuyawatu. He was a local Maasai tribesman who found a piece of translucent crystal near Mount Kilimanjaro. Fascinated by its blue-violet hue, he shared his find with Manuel D'Souza, a tailor by profession and prospector by passion, who was looking for rubies in the area. Many Africans tried a little mining on the side; Olengunin had almost blown himself up on one such venture.

Manuel D'Souza at first believed that they had found a vibrant sapphire, but the colour was more intriguing, alluring and exotic than any other gemstone. Henry B. Platt of Tiffany's named it *Tanzanite* after its country of origin. He was awed by the stone's exquisite beauty, saying that it was 'the most beautiful blue stone discovered in over 2000 years'. A thousand times rarer than diamonds, it is a gemstone variety of the mineral zoisite. The random presence of *vanadium* in the same vicinity under exacting geological conditions, more than 585 million years ago, created the environment for tanzanite's conception.

Known originally as Blue Zoisite, the original name was changed as it was thought to sound too much like the English word for *suicide*. According to Maasai folklore, the colour blue is sacred and spiritual, symbolizing new beginnings. Only women blessed with fertility, with the miracle of new life, have the honour of wearing blue. Since the discovery of tanzanite, a new tradition has evolved whereby Maasai chiefs give tanzanite to their wives on the birth of a baby in order to bestow upon the infant a healthy, positive and prosperous life.

As tanzanite was born in fire, lightning having removed the bronze colour to bring out the blue-violet, it is not surprising that lightning conditions have a great effect on the stone. This metamorphosis is truly remarkable, as amazing as his infinitely precious Thomasina, thought Domenico. Morning sunlight adds red, orange, or yellow, making the gem more purple. Overcast light adds blue or grey. Fluorescent light strengthens the blue, whilst halogen lights add sparkle and purple. The gem was alive with possibilities; it was enchanted. Thomasina had been bewitched at first sight. Domenico had chosen well; the large tanzanite stone was set in diamond triangles to symbolize strength. Thus masculine and feminine were mingled in one soul. These glorious gems of nature would delight Thomasina and be the emblem of eternal love.

Thus, with his ring, champagne, and a last-minute picnic hastily stuffed into his rucksack, Domenico walked up to Wuthering Heights, trying unsuccessfully to get a little ahead of Thomasina. He needed time to prepare the surprise, to be awaiting her on bended knee. But of course Thomasina knew precisely what Domenico was doing and was about to ask her. As she ascended to this deeply loved place, she amused herself by rehearsing her answer. It had taken Domenico many years to make this decision; he could be more indecisive than Hamlet. Much as he loved and needed her, he had felt that he simply could not cope with her full-time. Thomasina's mercurial nature both beguiled and troubled him. Could he cope with domestic life together? She was very beautiful, flirtatious, and complicated; he was inflexible, jealous, and selfish. In friendships, Thomasina was attracted to outsiders and the unbalanced, her 'otherness', felt an immediate affinity with disturbed souls. Domenico was sensitive and literary, but he did not believe in platonic friendships between men and women. Men, he said, always had a lustful agenda, albeit at first concealed. They were sexual predators and opportunists. Once he possessed Thomasina in marriage, he would guard her like a lion.

Thomasina did not agree with Domenico's attitudes but she accepted them and in many ways enjoyed his jealousy; it was an inevitable consequence of her desirability. She had always been attractive to men, able to disturb and seduce them without even trying. A close friend of her mother had commented: 'Thomasina is beautiful even when she is wearing a towel'. Even as a baby the consultant paediatrician had commented on her extraordinary beauty, as had the GP and the orthopaedic consultant. By the time she was six months old she already had many admirers within the medical profession; a string of pearls adorned her even then. Having been born with the congenital defect of talipes, her left foot required surgery, further treatment and monitoring until she was 16 years of age. Her mother still treasured a tiny blue shoe which she had worn at the age of 18 months, turned slightly inwards by her small foot. After learning to crawl and walk wearing orthopaedic boots, Thomasina had been delighted by her first pair of proper shoes - even though she spent most of her time playing barefoot and naked, like a figure from William Blake or Chagall. An ethereal child who never conformed: her first words were a sentence, 'I am a good baby' – which seemed to come from out of the blue.

As she teasingly caught up with Domenico, ready to consent to the man who didn't even have time to go down on bended knee, she thought that her mother was certain to bring that blue shoe to her daughter's wedding; she would carry it in her pearl handbag. As well as the wonderful ring, Domenico also had a card for Thomasina; it was inspired by Heathcliff and Catherine who were depicted together in the drawing on the front of the card. Ted Hughes and Sylvia Plath had shared a passion for the Brontës. They had referred to themselves as Heathcliff and Cathy, and written their respective poems on Wuthering Heights during a visit there. Ted and Sylvia had been in love, romantically in love in this exact spot: an ominous thought perhaps, bringing a threatening stormcloud over the desolate landscape. But as Thomasina gazed at the two trees, side by side, she experienced a kind of premonition. It was comforting, not disturbing.

Almost a year later, Domenico was living on an RAF base and enjoying evenings in the Officer's Mess, whilst Thomasina was completing the preparation for their wedding in Positano on May 13th 2010. She was still 'Cathy' but did Domenico remain as her 'Heathcliff'? A 39-year-old consultant psychiatrist named Dr Thackray Fitzroy was destined to assist her in uncovering identity, as well as accurately determining the number of ribs she had. He also offered therapy for her spider phobia. Perhaps he is going to hypnotize me, thought Thomasina, or administer a narcotic in the green tea they both enjoyed. Like Titania, she might 'wake when some vile thing is near' and fall in love at first sight. Thackray was always teasing her about the contents of his medi-bag; what magic might he perform with those powerful psychiatric drugs? His tablets and potions which altered the mind were surely akin to Oberon's love-juice 'on sleeping eyelids laid'. Concealed within Thackray's healing hands was a flower of purple dye, used by the King of Shadows to control perception: Thomasina was sure of this. Certainly, Thackray's male cat might have belonged to an alchemist or illusionist and been his Puck-like accomplice.

Thackray was unprepossessing in appearance, tall and slim, with fair hair of a ginger hue. His colouring clearly revealed an Irish ancestry from which he had resolutely distanced himself. His brief childhood encounters with relatives in Northern Ireland had horrified him. He was also repelled by his mother and dentist brother, from whom he was estranged.

Thomasina was a member of his mental health team in Manchester, and therefore a colleague. Although plain and rather geekily hunched over in appearance, conveying awkwardness, Thackray possessed a highly intelligent face and the manners of a perfect gentleman. He was rather snobbish and obsessively distanced himself from his appalling background, including the deranged, possessive mother, but seemed capable of empathy and friendship. Thomasina felt sorry for him; she thought that he was socially inept, inhibited and probably very lonely. He appeared, to her, to have a slight 'Lintonesque' quality. Was he capable of a grand passion such as that which united Heathcliff and Catherine, or only the tame indulgence of puppy love? Thomasina felt drawn to him, but purely as a sister.

Wuthering Heights is associated with the Earnshaws; for Heathcliff it *is* the wonderful Catherine and the beautiful side of their enduring love. Emily Brontë chose the name 'Wuthering' as a significant provincial adjective, descriptive of the atmospheric tumult to which its position exposed it in stormy weather.

Thrushcross Grange, the home of the refined, superficial and socially elevated Lintons, is only four miles from the Heights, but offers a complete contrast. It occupies a sheltered position on lower ground and is surrounded by lush vegetation and a high wall, implying confinement. The Grange is a place of boundaries and restrictions, pleasant at first but quickly suffocating. When the pampered Catherine lies ill in bed at the Grange, she thinks of her candlelit chamber at Wuthering Heights, and longs to return home.

Unfortunately for Catherine, she is in conflict with herself, torn between her love for Heathcliff, which resembles the eternal rocks, and her attraction to Edgar Linton who satisfies her desire for wealth and social position.

As Heathcliff and Catherine leave the freedom of childhood to enter their respective adult prisons, a transformation occurs. After Mr Earnshaw dies and Hindley inherits the estate, it becomes a place of ill treatment for Heathcliff. For Catherine, Thrushcross Grange is a respite from her alcoholic brother and his abuse of Heathcliff. At first it is all fine living and elegance, but later on she finds it stifling and her soul longs to be back at Wuthering Heights with Heathcliff.

Catherine seeks freedom through escape to the rocks and moors, especially Penistone Crags, which represent her love for Heathcliff. In the spring, flowers bloom among the gritstone outcrops and it becomes a place of beauty, signifying the innocence and spontaneity of childhood. In the second half of the book, young Cathy shows her affinity with her mother through her yearning to escape the confinement of the Grange and run free on the moors. She is forbidden by her father to go beyond the boundary walls of her home, but eventually the sheltered young Cathy falls in love with Hareton and the two discover the fairy cave at the foot of Penistone Crags. They go to this place to find some happiness.

'I am Heathcliff!' says Catherine; Heathcliff repeatedly calls Catherine his soul. According to C. Day Lewis, Heathcliff and Catherine 'represent the essential isolation of the soul, the agony of two souls or rather, shall we say, two halves of a single-soul – forever sundered and struggling to unite.' They are soul-mates, two people who have an affinity for each other which draws them together irresistibly. Because the relationship is of an ideal nature, it does not exist in life: this is why Catherine and Heathcliff often describe their love in impersonal terms. Catherine's conventional and limited feelings for Edgar Linton contrast with her profound love for Heathcliff, an assertion of identity based on the other. She tries to explain this to Nelly: '. . . surely you and everybody have a notion that there is, or should be, an existence of yours beyond you. What were the use of my creation if I were entirely contained here? My great miseries in this world have been Heathcliff's miseries, and I watched and felt each from the beginning; my great thought in living is himself. If all else perished, and he remained, I should still continue to be; and if all else remained, and he were annihilated, the universe would turn to a mighty stranger. I should not seem part of it.'

Heathcliff and Catherine attempt to transcend isolation by breaking down the boundaries of self to achieve fusion with another and create a unified identity. This need for fusion motivates Heathcliff's determination to 'absorb' Catherine's corpse into his and for them to 'dissolve' into each other so that Edgar will not be able to distinguish Catherine from him. Their love has a religious urgency and intensity. Echoing Cathy, Heathcliff says late in the book, 'I have nearly attained my heaven; and that of others is altogether unvalued and uncoveted by me!' Salvation is a private, eroticized aspiration.

Freud, on whom Thomasina had written her BA dissertation, understood this urge as an inherent part of life: 'At the height of being in love, the boundary between ego and object threatens to melt away. Against all the evidence of his senses, a man who is in love declares 'I' and 'you' are one, and is prepared to behave as if it were a fact.'

Extraordinarily, the Catholic wedding mass to which Thomasina had agreed as a concession to her future husband's denomination, emphasized the union of man and woman in marriage. Yet the institution of marriage was supposedly a reflection of Christ's relationship to his Church. Redemption, says Christianity, is attainable only through God. One cannot be redeemed solely through personal desire, imaginative power, or love for a human: ultimately we have our being in God.

For Catherine and Heathcliff, their calling is to be the '*other*'; their passion is mystical. They are devoted to empathy and are even willing to suffer death for the sake of this connection. They will ensure the mutilation of both social custom and the flesh in order to overcome separateness of existence. This desire for transcendence takes the form of crossing boundaries and rejecting conventions. Emily Brontë dissects uncontrolled passion, violence, sado-masochism, usurpation of property rights, imprisonment, and adultery, with hints of necrophilia and ghosts. When the dying Catherine says, 'I'm wearying to escape into that glorious world', she knows that her separation from Heathcliff is only temporary, as she will be reunited with him when his life on earth is ended. The fulfilment of their love after death is manifest in the account of the little boy having seen them after death, walking together on the moor.

Thackray Fitzroy seemed to be obsessed by boundaries; he lived a life enclosed. Not for him, apparently, an addictive love that wants to break down barriers of identity and merge with the lover. The 'loss' of his various girlfriends appeared to be entirely under his control. Having decided that the time had come to get rid of the current 'date', he simply sent an email listing their flaws. He would subsequently place them in his gallery and remember them fondly but critically. They had all been given similar advice for areas of improvement, and his descriptions revealed virtually identical biographies. 'A very nice girl, very pretty ... but it wasn't really working out.' To Thomasina, this bland process suggested a very limited capacity to lose control and fall in love. Despite his isolation he seemed very self-contained. She despaired of helping him to find a close companion.

It seemed to Thomasina that despite his expressed desire for a wife and three children; the loss of a lover would never cause him to suffer withdrawal symptoms. Thackray tried obsessively to photograph her, as though he was already framing the beautiful image to place it in the past. Although identified by him as a specific, overwhelming individual, she felt documented for a precious archive. The Thackray Fitzroy Collection: she denied it; she would *not* be photographed nor disappear. Or did he fear to cross boundaries because his love was lukewarm, or was he showing a capability of putting the needs of the beloved first? Thackray was an enigma.

Having intimately explored her perfectly formed body, Domenico concluded that Thomasina had in fact a strange imperfection – a missing rib! She knew that her grandma was always re-called after a chest x-ray because she had some sort of misalignment of a rib which caused a shadow on the screen. It is extremely difficult to ascertain the number of ribs a person has and usually a malformation causes no problem. Therefore an extra or missing rib usually passes unnoticed.

However, Thomasina had been poetically certain for many years now that she was in search of her missing rib, and that Domenico must be the one created from it! Thackray had promised to resolve the question by giving her a thorough examination. He asked her to lie down on his bed, as he did not own a sofa, and remove her jumper top. The carefully studious prodding and poking took some time, after which Thackray informed her that she did *not* have a missing rib, but a *depressed* rib, concave in form instead of convex. Unusual, he said and probably congenital. 'It will certainly mean something but I'm not sure what. I'll have to research it further.' He was in full Doctor mode, serious and arrogant, which always made Thomasina laugh. She had been worried that her strange rib might make her internal organs vulnerable. When she pointed anxiously at her 'heart' it was Thackray's turn to laugh. 'That's actually your liver,' he said smirking, adding that he couldn't imagine how all those organs fitted into that tiny, compact body.

As a pre-school child and beyond, Thomasina had been fascinated by hospitals. Her favourite toys had been her Fischer-Price medical kit, especially the stethoscope, and the Fisher-Price hospital. She would spend hours completely immersed in playing out elaborate medical scenarios, with dramatic encounters, operations and disappearances. She loved to hide her plastic figures behind the screens, and when she herself visited Addenbrooke's as a patient she enjoyed the ordered environment. Also, her Uncle Mark was a GP so there was medicine in the genes; and much of her working life was now spent in hospitals. It was a world she felt at home in, although the part of her that adored horseriding sometimes wanted to concentrate solely on horses. At present she rode every week but just didn't have the time for equine ownership. Having had her own pony in childhood, she knew how many hours a day had been devoted to *Amarilli*.

Thomasina loved animals and had grown up with quite a menagerie: three very special cats, a pair of gerbils named Oberon and Titania, a large terrifying hamster who opened his mouth very wide, her grandma's dogs, and, of course, her Welsh mountain mare, beautiful, moody and wilful. Thackray had a fascinating and very attractive male cat named Cato, who was suitably pampered. He always slept on the bottom of Thackray's bed and, like Thomasina's own Kambos, was rather a 'bruiser', affectionate one moment, biting and kicking the next. Cato had a lovely drinking fountain which Thackray had bought him for Christmas, but what made him unique was his propensity to have sex with Thackray's arm. He got astride, subdued the arm by biting into it and then began to vigorously 'hump', having dominated the 'female'. When Thackray told Thomasina that this behaviour was the reason he had decided to have Cato neutered, but in fact it had made no difference, she suggested that he might be a 'rigg'. As mentioned earlier, he was a 'puckish' feline. Cato and his human companion inhabited a vast, run-down Victorian end-of-terrace. Thomasina said that it evoked the spirits of *Psycho* and Miss Haversham! Thackray had, at last, got around to implementing improvements and had sought help from Thomasina when choosing his style of kitchen. With so many period features untouched, the enormous, near-empty house could eventually be spectacular. One of Thomasina's fantasies was the renovation of just such a place, so she was keen to advise. Thackray's fantasies were of a very different kind.

Being a psychiatrist, Thackray was inevitably slightly mad and this appealed to Thomasina. It was one of the reasons that she was so fond of him. She hoped he would prove to be an unconventional and interesting platonic friend, in addition to being a respected colleague. Certainly, they shared a quirky sense of humour, an enviable empathy. It was true that there seemed to be no particular thing in which they both felt interested, but Thomasina felt relaxed in his presence and Thackray said that she was 'very good company'. Somewhat circumspect she thought, but always the perfect gentleman in speech and manner.

With her wedding-day approaching Thomasina was preoccupied by last-minute preparations and a forthcoming 'burlesque' weekend in Bath with all her close female friends. Thackray was floundering in his relationship with his long-term girlfriend and had decided to call it a day. Thomasina thought she would cheer him up with a birthday cake for April 13th and advise him on a new 'dating' profile and strategy. Having expressed gratitude and appreciation for her offering and arranged to briefly meet up for green tea and cake, he cancelled …

Thomasina was baffled and disconcerted at this unexpectedly rude behaviour. He ignored her telephone calls and, when they spoke at last, gave evasive replies. Following a series of oblique answers, he finally admitted that his reason for this sudden change of behaviour was 'the need to set boundaries'. Baking a cake was perhaps 'inappropriate' for an engaged woman; like a Laura Ashley catalogue, it was a symbol of 'domesticity and commitment'.

A fortnight later, Thackray was still struggling with boundaries, although he assured her that their friendship remained intact. So she arranged to collect his proffered wedding present as well as some further things he wished to give her including a dressing-room screen. No cancelling was permitted! It was also an opportunity for her to see how his house renovation was progressing, and to return his emerald-green cashmere jumper. Thackray was delightful once he relaxed and lost his serious, impatient doctor's manner. Thomasina's former colleague, Jason, who had also worked with Thackray and was most perceptive, used to imitate his aloof, detached style with patients; saying typically: 'Sorry I can't help you with that or anything else. See you in three months.' When Thomasina asked Thackray how he coped with distressed patients in tears, he replied dismissively, though tongue-in-cheek, 'I usually roll my eyes and look at my watch'.

Thackray apologised yet again to Thomasina for having occasionally lost control of himself when in her presence. 'You shouldn't come round looking so sexy,' he said. 'I become overexcited.' Like your cat, Cato, thought Thomasina privately. It was at these moments that he became aware of the possibility of overstepping boundaries, admitted Thackray, but when they were actually together he was so happy in her company that all reservations disappeared. Thackray enjoyed changing persona. During a role-playing game which seemed to please him, he said that if Thomasina became his fiancée she could cease to work if she wished and have a horse plus £400 a week for herself. He would employ a cleaner and all he would expect of Thomasina was that she did the cooking and kept herself as pretty as possible for him. In some ways it was a tempting prospect! But Thomasina was passionately and wholly in love with her handsome, darling Domenico.

Thomasina had intended to invite Thackray and a 'friend' to her wedding-reception party in England, but she knew that he would decline. Who on earth would make a fitting consort for the strange, conflicted, struggling creature? Was he an utterly conventional Edgar Linton, confined and confining, or a fascinatingly unsettling hybrid like Marc Chagall's cat with a human face in *Paris Through the Window*? Thomasina's theme for Ilkley Moor was to be *Midsummer Dreamers*, Titania and her beloved Oberon, beyond male and female, a dream-spirit of pure libido. A forest bed-bower would be the focus of the evening's verdant sensuality. Chagall's 1939 *Midsummer Night's Dream* its portrait.

Midsummer Dreamers – Coda

How unstable is identity and love? How fickle are lovers? Is anyone really ready for marriage? Was everything to conclude in doubt?

The spell is broken. The visions disappear like a dawn mist. Everyone awakes and identities are resumed.

'Be as thou was wont to be.
See as thou was wont to see.
Wake, you thou my sweet Queen.'

New in amity the couple enjoy their first dance, but who will claim the fairy queen when the festivities are over?

Hand in Hand Domenico and Thomasina together take their leave.

Dream Wedding; May 13th 2010

The wedding guest, Praiano

The Amalfi Coast in Southern Italy is dream-laden and bewitched. Many famous novels and films have been inspired by the Bay of Naples and its associated coastline, whilst the nearby islands of Li Galli and Capri obsessed international artists and writers such as Rudolf Nureyev and Axel Munthe. The theme of this impossibly beautiful area has often been that of longing and transience, reflected in the movement of the sea and enchanted moments spent among ancient ruins. Green is the predominant colour of this lush and fertile landscape. Near-vertical limestone cliffs are adorned with tumbling cultivated terraces, the soil enriched by the power of earlier volcanic eruptions. Everywhere, the sight and taste of enormous oranges and sweet lemons, trailing grape vines, olives and figs, delight the senses. Exquisite fragrant wild flowers mingle with the abundant produce of hard-working farmers to create a scented arcadia. The blues of sea and sky express a serene rapture whilst the watching sun-god imbues all with intellect and sacred creativity. Man and his fellow creatures live in suspended ecstasy, somewhere between dream and reality.

To stand at midday on the *Terrace of Infinity* at Villa Cimbrone in Ravello, or stroke the flank of the *Parapet Sphinx* at Axel Munthe's Tiberian *Villa of San Michele* on Capri is to ascend to the realm of Zeus. Deified, one looks down on the earth below. The great writer Henry James, who often stayed at the Villa with his friend Munthe, described it as the most beautiful place in the world, a living example of *the dream that became reality*. 'The soul needs more space than the body,' wrote Munthe.

The May 13th wedding of Tamsin and Dominic was the incarnation of just such a vision. After months of planning, the marriage was finally solemnized at the Church of Santa Caterina in Positano, and the reception took place at Praiano, overlooking the seductive three-rocks of the Sirens and Capri's dramatic I Faraglioni. It is impossible to imagine a more beautiful or haunting setting, redolent with myth. The view across the water towards these islands is like passionately loving a distant artist.

During the long enchanted days before the wedding ceremony, a number of unforgettable excursions were made, including a visit to Anacapri, from which a chair-lift was taken to mount Solaro, the highest point on the magical island. There we all enjoyed a bottle of delicious chilled Prosecco, the Italian equivalent to champagne. At the foot of the departure point for the mountain lay the narrow terrace leading to Doctor Axel Munthe's villa. A distinguished Swedish physician, his original research had been on post-partum bleeding, but it was the medicine of the mind which truly attracted him. Having volunteered to serve with the Red Cross during World War I, and devoted himself to the poor of Naples during the cholera epidemic, he yearned for calm and solitude.

Villa San Michele has been described as a citadel of the soul – a shrine to Munthe's favourite god, *Hypnos*. The god of sleep was the divine brother of Thanatos, god of death, our inescapable fate. The benign power of *Hypnos* directly linked to *hypnosis* had allowed Axel Munthe to give rest and tranquillity to the dying soldiers of the First World War. Ironically, the Doctor was an insomniac; Henry James had suggested that Munthe write a memoir of Villa San Michele, as a cure for his insomnia: 'Nothing like writing a book for a man who could not sleep.' For Henry's brilliant suggestion Axel was eternally grateful.

The enigmatic physician's need to be alone was also intimately connected to his introspective, depressive nature: 'The need for solitude is understandable in a person whose profession and life-work mean constant listening.' There are two images of the god Hypnos in Munthe's Villa; it is probable that the Doctor saw himself as the incarnation of the god of sleep. In treating women patients, such as his close friend and companion, Queen Victoria of Sweden, Munthe held the balance of power through psychological means. 'Drugs are for the dying not for those who are to live,' he wrote.

Although the Doctor would readily resort to drugs like morphine to treat the terminally ill, or those in unbearable pain, he would not countenance the use of drugs to treat his own sleep problems. Instead, he turned to his first love, *music*. It was the single most important thing in Munthe's life; it provided the repose that he was able to give others through hypnosis. Song and music healed him and was an essential shared element of his relationship with Queen Victoria of Sweden. During their time together at San Michele they spent hours in the restored chapel performing Schubert. Victoria would provide piano accompaniment for Axel's fine baritone voice. Two of his male patients were Strindberg and Maupassant – the latter, having attempted to commit suicide by cutting his throat, died a year later in a mental asylum. It is possible that in addition to hypnosis, Dr Munthe had treated the great writers using music-therapy. The Doctor regarded birdsong as music, and one of his greatest achievements at San Michele was to purchase Mount Barbarossa as a sanctuary for the migrating birds he so loved. All his life Axel Munthe was a helper of the poor and a protector of animals. When not actually performing music in the chapel, he said that healing music still surrounded him through the ever-present birdsong. When Axel eventually became temporarily sun-blind, the music of the birds was even more precious to him.

Over most people the Villa San Michele casts a unique otherworldly spell, but it awakes a feeling of fear in some for whom it is a nightmare, an insane obsessive quest for light which is overtaken by the darkness and death of its very origins under the Emperor Tiberius.

Doctor Munthe was initially drawn to San Michele because of the charming little chapel, abandoned at the time, which was believed to stand on the site of one of Tiberias' twelve villas.

Rumour and primitive superstition surrounded these grounds. Villagers said that the missing bells of the small chapel would ring out as a sign that the Emperor was seeking forgiveness for having sentenced Christ to death.

Rooms within Villa San Michele display the Doctor's varied collections, ranging from classical antiquities to medieval and Renaissance sacred works. The atmosphere is one of culture and superstition. It is easy to imagine Munthe, as a pioneer of modern psychiatry, walking through this strange interior with Victoria on his arm and communicating with her both as personal physician and partner in music. Axel's roman-style courtyards, marble walkways and atriums decorated with relics, confirm this haunting vision. Their ghosts are seen from the corner of one's eyes. They glide by noiselessly and are gone.

After admiring all Munthe's work of rebuilding the chapel and house, a project lasting more than five summers, we returned to his bedroom for another look at the bronze *Hypnos*, placed on a column beside Munthe's fifteenth-century Sicilian wrought-iron bed. The beautiful statue induces us to think of psychoanalysis and Munthe's therapeutic purpose. The second image of *Hypnos* is found in the open air Sculpture Gallery; it is close beside the *Resting Mercury*, messenger of the gods and guide of souls to the afterlife.

It was on the site of the old chapel of San Michele, that Munthe first conceived the idea of a house 'open to the sun and wind and the voices of the sea, like a Greek temple, and light, light, light everywhere.' In contrast, sepulchral items are everywhere in the Villa to remind us of darkness and its conflict with light. Munthe often worked alone in the garden by moonlight. He attempted to reconcile Hypnos and Thanatos, but he was always seeking the glory of the sunlight that he so loved. Munthe's creations pose many unanswered questions. Peter Cottino, the current curator of Villa San Michele, has described it as 'a place for you who yearn, dream and search for answers'. He also draws poignant attention to the parallels between Axel Munthe and Icarus, as a man who in looking for the light was later 'violently driven into the shadows, blind and alone'.

Our Italian wedding journey offered many more joys, thrills, Roman and Greek antiquities, and unforgettable views. The wedding party being applauded, and the bride and groom being photographed as they walked the narrow cobbled streets and steep steps of Positano made the spirit soar. After the perfect meal and sublime lemon wedding-cake, made especially in Amalfi, we concluded our blessed revels in the piazza of the Basilica San Gennaro where the sea serves as its lovely backdrop. The delightful musicians walked with us, continuing to play on the guitar and mandolin as sky-lanterns were released. A final reading of the Britten/Purcell love-offering *Sweeter than Roses* took place in the illuminated piazza in front of San Gennaro. Just as the words of the beautiful song were at an end, the bells of the great church sounded midnight – the wedding day was over but always to be remembered. Who could ever forget the music of Bach and Vivaldi, the blessing and exchanging of rings or the solemn vows in front of the magnificent marble altar, adored with baroque cherubs? The bride and groom looked so beautiful and happy that it seemed we were witness to a dream.

Lilac, purple, blue and gold were their heavenly colours shining forth from the stained-glass windows above the altar and the tanzanite-and-diamond ring of the bride in the light-filled chapel. The yellow-gold braid and blue of the groom's RAF uniform made its own unique contribution to the sense of Paradise in the sacred union between this man and this woman:

'I gaze at you, I possess you,
I clasp you, I entwine you.
No more pain, no more death,
O my life, my treasure.

I am yours, I am yours,
My joy, say you love me too.
You are my idol, you alone,
Indeed, my love, my life, indeed,
…the treasure of my heart…'

> *Pur ti miro*, final duet from
> Claudio Monteverdi,
> *L'Incoronazione di Poppea (1607)*

Thinking on all this, the corner of Axel Munthe's chapel loggia came to mind, where sits the famous *Egyptian Sphinx*, more than 3,200 years old. Seated on the terrace parapet overlooking the entire Bay of Naples, we are unable to see its face – frustrating but deliberate of course. Henry James called this Villa and garden 'the most fantastic beauty, poetry and inutility that one had ever seen clustered together', with the sphinx as its symbol.

It is said that if you touch the sphinx's hindquarters with your left hand while making a wish it will come true. Standing high up on this rocky ledge at the foot of Mount Barbarossa, listening to the birdsong, there was only one wish devoutly to be made – that the young bridal couple remain forever in this Eden – this little realm of the gods:

'Was it a vision, or a waking dream?
Fled is that music: -
Do I wake or sleep?'
John Keats – *Ode to a Nightingale* c.1884

*   *   *

Henry James was right! The two most evocative and beautiful words in the English language are 'Summer Afternoons'. That thought, which he had described so long ago, at the very beginning of the twentieth century, was singularly apt for this perfect scene now being enacted on 26th June, close to the time of Midsummer day 2010, on the lush lawns of a former Catholic retreat in Yorkshire.

The day was gloriously hot; the sun shone beneficently from a clear blue sky. Individual trees shimmered in the heat, whilst the adjacent green wood looked cool and inviting. A backcloth of golden wheat fields rose up behind the ancient house, shining like a holy gift. The two small children playing in their sandpit beneath the Elizabethan mullioned windows added to the sense of inhabiting an Eden.

Little Cecelia, aged three years and six months resembled a renaissance angel with Leonardoesque hair in tendrils, and had been named after the martyred patron saint of music. Her toddler brother, Benedict, had blond curly hair and dark brown eyes; he was a living baroque cherub. Both children were utterly enchanting to watch, their games occasionally interrupted by the wafting past of huge, clumsy Bramley, the family's long-haired golden retriever. He always wanted to be included in everything and kept trying to attract attention by bringing his ball and repeatedly dropping it at the feet of anyone he could find. On such a scorching day as this he had to be hosed down, although it took many minutes before the water penetrated his dense coat. Having found temporary relief from the heat he would run past the children, almost knocking them over, and then lie sprawled out on the stone balustrade. Benedict was already adept at avoiding Bramley as he hurtled around the garden, quickly sidestepping when the dog gambolled towards him, and throwing out his chubby arms in protest if the enormous animal crossed his path. Cecelia was more accommodating towards her huge furry friend, although she became upset when he stole the sweets which she was just about to place in her mouth. Her food obsessed little brother had once eaten Bramley's dog food. He had crawled over to the large bowl, scooped up the meaty contents and started to feed himself. Fortunately his mother had quickly noticed what was happening, but Cecelia had thought it only fair that the dog should know what it felt like to have his food suddenly snatched away from him - after all Bramley had stolen her delicious 'Percy Pig' sweets, which Mummy had bought her from M&S.

Cecelia and Benedict's toddler cousin Nancy joined them in the sandpit after her midday sleep. Her baby-blond ringlets and ethereal grace were fairylike. The onlookers thought her akin to the beautiful butterflies which had settled on the nearby flowers. At only 18 months she had already mastered the basics of the English language and was able to tell Benedict to stop emptying the sandpit and share his toys. Like many firstborn children she was very advanced when it came to communication, and an awareness of hazards. Unlike Benedict, who was oblivious to walking barefoot on thistles, both Cecelia and Nancy complained and demanded their shoes.

On that idyllic afternoon in the midsummer of 2010 there were four generations enjoying the serene aftermath of the previous evening's wedding celebrations beneath a full moon. All except the small children intent on their games relished the spectacular view from the elevated country house. The large gardens ended in a high stone wall, but enjoyed an uninterrupted panorama over the small town of Ilkley below and the high moor beyond. 'If there is an afterlife, then let it be on earth, for truly *this* is paradise', said the mother-of-the-bride to Anthony, her charming host of Irish descent and the master of the house. The tall and handsome Anthony surveyed his south facing antique property and glorious grounds; it was clear that his delightful little son would one day resemble him exactly. They shared the same wonderful mop of curls, dark expressive eyes and commanding presence. At only 18 months Benedict already had a magnificent confident posture and manner, which exuded authority and charisma. Looking at photographs of father and son as infants, it was almost impossible to tell them apart.

The children's adoring maternal grandmother looked upon the sunlit scene with immense satisfaction. She was deeply proud of her lovely firstborn daughter, Lucy, now a devoted mother of two as well as a loving wife and mistress of Myddelton House. Lucy had always been exceptionally clever and the light of her mother's life, but having met, fallen in love with, and married Anthony at a relatively early age, it had seemed a long time before their marriage was blessed with children. Susan enjoyed every moment of her role as grandma, her incredible drive and energy found a most rewarding outlet in her three grandchildren, and her second daughter, Sarah, also gifted with high intelligence was due to give birth in just two weeks. Soon there would be four grandchildren, including a newborn baby to fit into her busy schedule. Despite her demanding childcare commitments she was still doing her nursing shifts in Leeds. But Susie was always happy to stay-over at Lucy and Anthony's; the place was a restorative for both mind and body.

Despite the remote location of Myddelton, and its turbulent history as a stronghold for Catholic recusants refusing to submit to the authority of the Church of England, it exuded protectiveness and serenity. Lucy and her family felt further reassured by having had the house blessed by their local Bishop. When, some months later Susie had experienced a strange dream, or haunting in the bedroom where she always slept, the local priest had sprinkled holy water in the 'disturbed' room and placed a photograph there of the Archangel Michael. Since this rite has been performed there had been no further encounters with the ghostly woman at the foot of Susie's bed, and no more strange, unexplained noises and sensations of cold.

Given the stories of Myddelton's importance over the centuries as a sanctuary for persecuted Catholics it is not surprising that it seemed haunted by the past. It was as important to the history of Yorkshire Catholicism as

Fountain's Hall and Abbey, described so memorably by Alan Bennett as 'a place free from all imperfection.' Fountains was also bound up with the life of the mother–of–the–bride, celebrating her daughter's Italian wedding at an English reception at the catholic retreat, followed by a midsummer barbecue on the lawns of Myddelton Lodge.

For the literary people present that afternoon there was a strong feeling of entering Gloriani's garden in Henry James *The Ambassadors*; Lucy and the mother-of-the-bride discussed these feelings when they visited the disused and neglected stone summerhouse at the bottom of the garden, one of several 19th century additions to Myddleton Lodge. Having both read English at University they fantasized that the deserted summerhouse could be restored as a writers' retreat. The place worked on their imaginations. But when the practical and energetic Susie entered the building, she noticed only the damp and decay. She found nothing magical there; it was simply an urgent building project. But it was Susie who had the flair and talent to convert the dream into reality, to create beauty and usefulness.

Meantime, the men had abandoned the barbecue which Anthony had lit and nurtured. The England game had started in the World Cup, so all the males including the new husband and his wife's younger brother, who had created such a memorable slide-show the previous evening, vanished into the lounge to watch the television coverage. Only the father-of-the-bride, a patient scientist remained outside to supervise the barbecue. His splendid sausages were greatly admired and enjoyed. The ladies had done all the preparation of the delicious food, so they went into the enormous kitchen to create a dessert leaving only the bride's grandmother outside on a sun-lounger, soon joined by the little children. Her miniature wire-hair dachshund Torah dozed nearby, contented in the shade.

Dear Anthony and Lucy were the perfect host and hostess, ensuring that their guest of nearly ninety was happy and comfortable in the shade, beneath the kitchen window. Anthony had provided a luxurious lounger with cushions and a small table for drinks. Lucy kept brewing tea and taking out glasses of lightly fruited water to 'great-grandma', so that she did not become dehydrated. Nobody could have been more kind or attentive than Lucy, her sister, and their mother.

Very soon the little group in the kitchen had finished making the Eton mess and were ready to serve a late lunch to the gentlemen in the lounge. As they put the finishing touches to the broken meringue, they noticed the heads of the children bobbing up and down outside the kitchen window. Concerned as ever for the well-being of the nearly ninety year old, Lucy called to her to ask if all was well. 'Yes, we're having a wonderful time' shouted the elderly lady and Cecelia, whilst Benedict gurgled his pleasure in exploring the grandma of his newly-wed uncle, his mother's adored younger brother. Cecelia was enjoying looking at 'great-grandma's' jewellery and talking to her about all the things that she wanted to show her. Benedict just loved sliding, jumping and being cuddled. His cool, velvet soft limbs were surprisingly strong and he found an ideal jumping platform on the prone body of the elderly lady, who had once been a primary school teacher much loved by her class of infants. Her empathy with the young had been a lifelong possession.

The remarkable afternoon spent at Myddelton Lodge and its surroundings would remain in her memory forever. After the exciting but exhausting revelries of the previous evening she had felt very happy, but tired. The party had been immensely enjoyable and it had been wonderful to see her beloved grand-daughter in her exquisite wedding-gown, but having left early she had missed the sky-lanterns and fireworks. This ecstatic summer afternoon in Lucy and Anthony's garden surrounded by loving family members had truly been the 'icing-on-the-cake'. She hoped to return one day; Anthony and Lucy had told her that she would always be welcome at their house. Next time she came to this joyful home she looked forward to exploring the tranquil woodland walks behind the house where a line of wooden carvings of the Stations of the Cross followed Christ's route to the tomb. This seemed an entirely appropriate setting for a devout Catholic like Anthony; he had recently been honoured with a Papal Knighthood for his services to Charity. The modern Catholic retreat, built in the 1960s was next door to his Grade 1 listed property and allowed constant contact with a valuable catholic institution which helped young people.

Anthony had been both shocked and amused when a drunken fight had broken out during the midsummer party at the retreat. In spite of highly visible portraits of saints and the Pope, this had not prevented one or two of the mainly Catholic guests from becoming involved in a nasty outbreak of violence. Fortunately, some of the groom's very large Yorkshire friends had intervened before things became too serious. Anthony's tongue-in-cheek comment was: 'We're still primitive in Yorkshire. It's not like down south. We still have punch-ups up here, even in front of pictures of the Pope!'

As the small group of family and friends made their preparations for the journey home, the sunset angelus bell magically sounded, announcing the Roman Catholic devotion commemorating the incarnation. The adults no linger cared that England had lost their football match and would now make the exodus home from South Africa in disgrace. The small children said their goodbyes with hugs and kisses, and were whisked away for bath-time and stories. The guests dispersed. Some weeks later on July 31st, Sarah's second daughter, Harriet Lucy was born. She shared her birth date with that of Joan Adelaide Elliott, the elderly lady who had been lying on the sunlounger one midsummer afternoon in the glorious garden overlooking Ilkley Moor. As baby Harriet

Lucy came into the world, Joan Elliott was happily celebrating her 90th birthday amidst family and friends.   Said Henry James' Lambert Strether in Gloriani's garden:

'Live all you can; it's a mistake not to'.

The   Ambassadors, 1903

A Note on Asclepius

Asclepius

    It was a boy, son of the beautiful mortal Coronis and the god Apollo, whom Apollo named Asclepius because he had been cut from his mother's womb. His mother suffered death for being unfaithful to Apollo and was laid on a funeral pyre to be consumed by fire, but the unborn child was rescued from her womb. From this he received the name Asclepius 'to cut open'. His divine father, Apollo, carried him off to the Cave of Cheiron the Centaur where he learned the Art of Medicine. Cheiron instructed him in surgery, the interpretation of dreams, and the use of drugs. He became so skilled that he is revered as the founder of Medicine. His curative herb was mistletoe, thought by the ancient Greeks to be the genitals of the oak tree. The mistletoe was cut from the tree and the viscous juice of its berries, known as oak-sperm, was used as a sacral liquid of great regenerative virtue. Oberon's narcotic 'love-juice', derived from his flower of purple-dye in Shakespeare's *A Midsummer Night's Dream*, is a variation of this belief. The King of Shadows streaks the sleeping eyelids of lovers to alter their thoughts and emotions in his enchanted forest. Titania, his fairy Queen, sleeps on a magical bank amidst luscious flowers and the enamell'd skin of snakes.

The rod of Asclepius, a snake-entwined staff, remains a symbol of Medicine today, usually in its derivative form of the winged Caduceus, which the god Hermes/Mercury also carries. Antinous, the beautiful Greek youth and beloved of the Emperor Hadrian was made a god after his tragic drowning in the River Nile; his commemorative statuary often depicts him as a healing deity with Caduceus. The most famous Temple of Asclepius was at Epidauros in the Peloponnese, where non-venomous snakes were used in curative rituals. The snakes were allowed to crawl on the floor where the sick and injured slept. Dreaming, whilst in the presence of snakes, was regarded as especially beneficial. Any visions would be reported to a priest who would prescribe the appropriate therapy by a method of interpretation.

Hippocrates, who served in the famous healing temple of Kos, was thought to have been a descendent of Asclepius. The original ancient Hippocratic Oath begins with the invocation: 'I swear by Apollo the Physician and by Asclepius and by Hygieia and Panacea and by all the gods ...' A number of stories say that Zeus killed Asclepius with a thunderbolt as a punishment for bringing people back from the dead. Hades was no longer receiving spirits into the Underworld, so was angered. After Asclepius' death, Zeus placed him among the stars as the constellation *Ophiuchus* – the Serpent Holder. He is, thereby, eternally exalted.

Floatershell
The Haunting of Julius Kandel

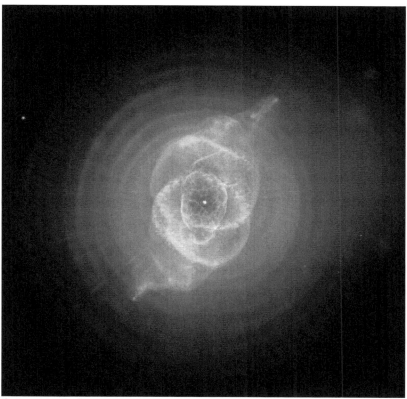

Cats-eye nebula

"He who has seen a ghost, cannot be as if he had never seen it." - John Henry Cardinal Newman

The Lancet: Obituary-

The eminent physician did not come from an advantaged background, yet he rose to the top of his profession. A lifelong interest in the human eye became almost obsessional after his mother was ravaged by brain disease and blindness. Like Algeron Blackwood, the supernaturalist and intellectual mystic, he believed in an empathy between man and the elemental powers that are apart from, yet within man. From the earliest stages of his mother's illness, young Julius relentlessly studied perception as the key to reconciling 'spirit and matter'. He was convinced that science and imagination work symbiotically to form the mind's vision, to reveal what he termed 'the terror and beauty of the Universe.' Quantum mechanics and general relativity have led to a different way of thinking about matter than that implied by conventional observation. In particular, quantum mechanics has resulted in perceived paradoxes in measurement and observation, which have led some scientists to question the nature of reality. Julius was often afraid of what might be there, that he could not see, but also of his capacity to see what is possibly not there at all. Interpenetrating dimensions of existence must be the answer to this mystery, thought Julius. Some members of the conservative scientific establishment dismissed his preoccupations as wayward, irrational 'fantasies', powered by a longing to conquer mortality. Treatment at *The Priory* clinic for what was described as 'a psychotic episode', almost derailed Julius' medical career, Certainly, the death of his beloved mother, when Julius was only 16, affected him deeply; he was vulnerable in relationships and retained an intense privacy. He found it very difficult to trust people; even his friends and colleagues found him remote, demanding and aloof. Also Julius' theories attracted controversy and jealousy. However, although he will be remembered for his strange aura of impenetrable loneliness, his uncanny brilliance in treating and understanding 'visual disorders of the eye and mind', ensures that the reputation of this psychic surgeon will long outlive his untimely passing into a world of shadows.

*   *   *

He would never forget his first terrifying encounter with the indistinct shape, as it moved slowly across the distant woodland clearing near his small village. The ghostly memory was imbued with the intensity of early childhood. He had come to the place quite by chance, as he wandered lost amidst the birch trees. To his horror, he at once named the object a *floatershell*, because it appeared to have an outline which hosted something.

The time had reached mid-afternoon in the mid-summer of 1957. The heat was palpable and his legs felt tired from aimlessly walking for so many hours. He knew that his mother would be expecting him home for tea and her anxiety would mount once the grandfather clock struck six and shadows began to fall. Also, his boyish appetite craved the lovely food which awaited him.

All the paths through the woods near his affluent village on the Hertfordshire and Essex border were familiar to him; he could not understand how he had missed his route home. He had taken some of his first toddler steps beside a great oak tree, but not until his sixth birthday would his mother allow him to explore alone beyond the garden gate. In the 1950s, the decade into which he was born, children were far less restricted than in the late twentieth and early twenty-first century. There were no home computers, mobile phones and electronic games, so children played mostly outdoors. Their main toys were bicycles, go-karts and the natural world.

Julius loved the old trees which edged the stream at the bottom of his large garden. They represented a changing fairy realm into which he could leap and disappear whenever he wished. He enjoyed searching there for fox-holes, badger burrows, and owl pellets. Julius looked upon these animals as his dearest and closest friends; their little lives inhabited his own waking and sleeping thoughts throughout the seasons. They meant more to him than any of his human companions, and this prime, sometimes painful, identification with non-human life would remain with him always. Unsurprisingly, his favourite book was *The Wind in the Willows*; he thought of himself as Mole. Julius also worshipped birds and bats; he never tired of watching them from his flat-roof house extension, at sunset. His bedroom window was large, and always left ajar in the hope that an owl or bat might fly in. Julius often climbed out of his bedroom at dawn, reaching the back lawn via the flat roof, and a convenient drainpipe which he shinned down. In this way he could enter his 'night-garden' without disturbing his parents and older sister Elyot who slept at the front of the house. Julius alone had the view across the woods and distant fields to yet more trees, culminating in a gloomy spinney of evergreens. His mother's climbing roses lined his magical path, all the way to the stream which marked his garden boundary.

No matter where young Julius rambled, he had always felt safe – until the appearance of the spectral shape in the clearing. Without waiting to see whether or not it was coming closer, he had screamed and run away as fast as he could. Tripping and stumbling, he had blindly followed a well-marked path until he finally discovered an exit point which took him to his nearby market-town of Bishop's Stortford. It was a very long and tiring walk home from this point of safety, but he did not care. He decided that he would walk any number of weary miles as long as he did not have to re-enter the dreaded wood, or pass the now threatening clearing. In England it is the Fen or Marsh which is the usual abode of ghosts, such as William Blake's *Little Boy Lost*. Perhaps the spectre in the wood had wandered over from the Cambridgeshire Fens, thought the traumatised boy.

Julius knew that his journey home was safe and that he was no longer lost, but his heart pounded in his small chest; he still felt menaced by that near-spherical, greyscale shape. In his imagination it seemed to be moving closer, coming towards him like a disembodied eye. Just visible through the outlet membrane was a grainy structure like a living creature enclosed within the floating mist ball.

By the time Julius reached his front door he felt less agitated, and when he sat at the old familiar dining table enjoying his meal with jelly and chocolate cake to follow, his tension finally drifted away. It was a lovely warm evening; there was nothing to fear. Soon he would have his bath, then do a complicated jigsaw, and after kneeling to say his prayers, get into bed with his favourite bear, Timothy, and secretly read by torchlight beneath his blanket. He always slept with his door slightly open as he felt comforted by the landing light and the proximity of family sounds from downstairs. He felt almost certain that the mysterious orb or ball of light had not observed him, and would never return.

In the winter of 1964 Julius was looking forward to his thirteenth birthday, and hoping for snow on the actual day. All his friends would be coming over for a party, and hopefully games in the snow to follow. Recently, it had been very cold and Julius always remembered to feed his animal companions. With the passing of time he had learned many facts about the natural world. Sadly, he realised that the pair of blackbirds nesting every year in his holly hedge, were probably not the original pair from his infancy, but his increased knowledge of natural history was also something to relish. Just recently in a biology lesson he had dissected a cow's eye. He felt uncomfortable about the death of the animal but was utterly fascinated by this organ of sight. Biology and English were his best subjects, but he was clever at everything so had decided to become a vet or a doctor. However, the consequences of a minor riding accident soon focused his talents in a more specialised direction.

At the age of six he had been obsessed with horse-riding and attempting to resurrect animals; he longed to understand the interface between life and death. His parents had noticed that he was a morbid boy who adored cemeteries and Boris Karloff films. Even during his earliest years, Julius had always identified with outsiders and any creature with a problem. Consequently, he was determined to befriend the nervous pony at the riding school, the mount that everyone avoided. She was a temperamental flea-bitten grey pony named Tamora. Julius had ridden her many times in the indoor school, and had learned to jump with her when his skills progressed. His teacher had decided that the time had come for Julius to take the mare along the country lanes, bridlepaths and open fields.

All went well for many weeks until the unfortunate incident with the backfiring motorbike. Julius and Tamora were happily cantering around a beautiful meadow when out of the blue there came a roar followed by a loud explosion. This sudden bang spooked both pony and rider. Julius lost his balance as Tamora bolted and, slipping from the saddle, he was carried across the field hanging by his left foot which had caught in its stirrup. From his alarming upside-down predicament Julius tried to arch his body and keep his bare head away from the ground and the pony's galloping hooves. The sudden jolt had dislodged Julius' riding hat; in those days the cork and velvet 'hunting caps' were only held on by a ridiculous elastic strap. In the event of an accident the first thing you lost was your useless head protection. Tamora had also pulled the reigns from the boy's hands so he had no control whatsoever. The pony sped around the field several times before Julius' tearful riding teacher was able to catch her, calm her down and rescue Julius.

He was badly shaken and very upset but sure that he had not hit his head. With the teacher's encouragement, he remounted his nervous pony, but he felt betrayed by her. He continued to choose her for lessons but his confidence and trust had been shattered. Nonetheless, when Julius later developed 'floaters' in both eyes and was packed off for a consultation with an ophthalmic surgeon, the onset of these moving grey shapes was ascribed to a head injury. His parents put it down to the incident with Tamora, but Julius knew that his head had touched neither hooves nor ground. The cause was much more likely to have been an earlier very nasty climbing-frame accident at primary school. During the lunch hour, Julius loved to play on the high frame, showing off to all his friends and the younger children. The metal climbing frame had no mats beneath and was very slippery in wet weather. During lunchtime all the teachers sat inside the school drinking tea and chatting. They locked the school doors so that they would not be disturbed. When Julius fell head first from the very top bar and saw stars, his friends rushed him to the school door and banged on the windows. At first the teachers motioned angrily for them to go away, but the children persisted. Julius was temporarily unable to swallow and the gravel from the playground was embedded in his cut knees. Eventually his class teacher appeared and she sent him into the cloakroom to have his wounds cleaned and bandaged by the dinner lady. When Julius told the teacher what had happened and that he was seeing stars and could not swallow properly, she said that if he told his mother about the accident he would be in very serious trouble both at home and at school. So Julius never spoke about his terrifying fall; he kept it a secret. His hatred of the teacher remained with him forever; he wanted her to die.

Eventually, Julius' brain became accustomed to these inhabitants of his eyes. There was one especially large 'floater' in his left eye which came to seem like a living thing, visible only to Julius and his eye specialist, but one adjusts and adapts, mused the child. It was part of the miniature world within him and inspired his decision to become a consultant ophthalmologist. He kept this ambition to himself, but the study of eyes was a passion. Julius himself had remarkable eyes; they were the chief beauty of his face inherited from his dark-skinned, black-haired, green-eyed father. Every adult commented admiringly on his huge dark-green orbs flecked with brown. His uncle described them as 'a light to civilisation'. Julius did not fully understand the meaning of this phrase but thought that it sounded amazing! When asked about the 'floaters' Julius lied, saying that he no longer noticed them. In fact, he looked upon them as his secret companions, part of his private inner world, through which he would gain knowledge.

The boy was well aware of the scientific explanation for these small pieces of debris that 'floated' in the vitreous humour of his eyes, but because his ghostly sighting in the wood had pre-dated the rational explanation for these shadows on his retina, he could never really separate the scientific from the supernatural, or other-worldly. What he had witnessed in the eerie clearing and what appeared cobweblike behind his clear lens, had somehow combined in his perception.

Julius knew that the object amongst the trees had not been an optical illusion but neither had it been a projection of the clouds within the vitreous jelly of his eyes. The shape in the clearing had its own autonomous existence, but when Julius first noticed his floaters, of so many different shapes and sizes, he wondered if they were a sign that the woodland orb would return one day. Perhaps, without warning it might appear at the top of the stairs, or come even closer on his landing just beyond his bedroom door. He sometimes felt that the harmless floaters were a deliberate reflection of the mysterious shape by which he was menaced. Was it possible that something benign might be linked to an invasive threat? This disturbing thought increased his childhood preoccupation with decay and regeneration.

Like Dr Frankenstein, he set himself the task of creating something living from something which had died. He had heard the story of Lazarus at his Church-of-England primary school and always believed that he must have resembled Boris

Karloff's Im-Ho-Tep, the mummy, revived after 3700 years by a British archaeology team. Julius watched the 1932 film again and again, loving the moment when the heavily bandaged Im-Ho-Tep, opens his eyes and returns to life! Karloff's large, brooding, melancholy eyes resembled his own. Julius' village school had profoundly affected him. The outlook there was feudal and narrow, with the emphasis on Christianity. The overpowering Scottish headmistress put religious observance at the top of the curriculum; she was hand-in-glove with the local vicar who called in almost daily. He usually attended both morning hymns and afternoon prayers. His outlook was High Anglican; the children were told that God was always watching them. The feudal outlook and rigid hierarchy still prevailed in Julius' village. New College, Oxford, owned much of the land, including the beautiful ancient flint church and its living. New College appointed the vicar, and the vicar controlled the school. The village gentry were still very much in control, and their sons and daughters went to Oxbridge to read either Medicine or Law. The Establishment was still running the village, and although London commuters were now living there (Julius' father included), there was still very little social mobility in the 1950s and early 1960s. The ordinary local people had narrow horizons and were mostly content to live in council houses or tithe cottages. Their children attended the nearby secondary modern school and returned to employment within the village. The wealthy farmers and professional people did not send their children to the village school; they were educated privately and given every advantage. Julius rebelled against this blinkered system, but enough of school ritual had entered his soul to compel him to 'pour libations' to appease the gods. He sometimes made 'offerings' of his precious sweets, throwing them on the ground, even though he longed to eat them rather than thus deprive himself. But having assuaged the anger of the Deity, the small boy felt that he would not now be punished by blindness. One of the reasons he always slept with a torch underneath his pillow was to check his eyesight during the night-time. Religious guilt, once implanted, is very difficult to erase; it is the probable cause of the many sightings of a monk in the Cistercian ruins of Fountains Abbey, despoiled at the time of the Reformation.

As he grew towards adolescence, Julius became especially close to nocturnal predators, like cats, owls and bats; these were the animals which now fascinated him most of all. He admired their heightened sensory perception and its use in hunting. Whilst still at primary school, he had experimented on small dead birds and rodents, placing them carefully in an air-tight tin after wrapping them in bandages and burying them beneath the earth in his own little garden plot. Within days he would dig them up, observe their state of decay, and then re-bury them, for subsequent repeated exhumation. He wrote down all his observations, hoping that one day he might have the knowledge to revive his little friends. He always tried to protect the birds from his beloved pet cats, but when a rescued bird subsequently died from injury or shock, he always cradled it in his hands and felt heartbroken when its eyes finally closed in death. He had saved and rehabilitated many animals but was deeply grieved when his intervention failed.

In the autumn term of 1965, when Julius was 14, he received a spectacular school report. He knew that he had studied incredibly hard and was on the way to reading medicine in the near future. He had won the school science prize for a project on human sight, with special reference to *subjective vision*. As part of his dissertation he had naturally explored the perception of floaters, known as *myodesopsia*. Studies showed that these deposits were of 'various size, shape, consistency, refractive index, and motility within the eye's vitreous humour, which is normally transparent.' Julius learned that they could be of embryonic origin due to the disintegration of the hyaloid artery during the foetal stage of development in the third trimester of pregnancy, or acquired later due to degenerative changes of the vitreous humour or retina. One specific fact embedded itself in Julius' mind: 'Since these objects exist within the eye itself, they are not optical illusions but are entoptic phenomena.' In some uncanny way the *floatershell* which he had glimpsed on that far off summer evening, resembled the shapes now suspended in the vitreous humour of his eyes. So had that been the explanation for the sighting of the slightly blurry, unstable image? Julius had not been aware at that time that his eyes contained these drifting, changeless cells, known as 'floaters', but perhaps he had mistaken his own suspended protein specks for the sickening object in the clearing? There must be a scientific theory to explain all this.

Julius often tried to reassure himself by lying supine beneath a bright-blue sky, and deliberately focussing on the large masses, which would remain in his field of vision for a lifetime. Rather than trying to ignore them, he decided to enjoy them at their most prominent. Even when he closed his eyes, the intense light made them seem to drift constantly as projected shadows. They would never become invisible; they would always be in close proximity to his retina, probably growing larger and darker. During a recent check-up with the ophthalmologist he had been able to observe his floaters much more closely. The specialist had used a slit lamp; increasing background illumination and using a pinhole to decrease pupil diameter had enabled Julius to enjoy a conspicuous view and sharpened image of the fibrous elements within his floaters. This detailed representation of the debris inside the watery-jelly of his vitreous humour which fitted his eyeball, unnerved Julius. It unlocked a most disturbing memory from the shadowy woodland clearing, a memory which could not be repressed and had affected him deeply. He knew that the *floatershell* had been coming closer and that something deep inside it had been trying to observe him, perhaps recording his time on earth. Presumably it had failed to accomplish this task; Julius had managed to escape from its presence – the only reminder being the particles inside his wonderful dark-green, golden-flecked eyes. But Julius felt unpleasantly scrutinised.

After all the excitement of the school prize-giving when Julius had been singled out for his exceptional intellectual gifts, he was happy to roll into bed early and dream of his future in science and medicine. He switched off his lamp and gazed sleepily at the softly illuminated landing. He fell asleep almost at once but awakened suddenly at first light. He felt that he wanted to rise immediately from his bed; it was an overwhelming impulse. As he tried to sit up he realised that his body was paralysed. He could raise his head, but that was all. Helplessly immobile, he wondered if, in fact, he was still asleep. But no, he was entirely conscious and alert. Something had disturbed him. He had been woken by a deep, masculine voice calling to him. It had said only one word, very distinctly: the single word had been 'Tallia'. Julius knew enough about the human body to realise that his temporary paralysis was due to a sudden fall in blood pressure. It was a very rare but harmless occurrence, probably a once-in-a-lifetime event. He glanced helplessly across the landing to the top of the stairs; his sister's bedroom was adjacent to the stairwell. As he raised his head to look again at the far-landing window he sensed a greyscale presence moving towards him.

Helplessly prone on his bed, Julius screamed…but no sound came from his wide opened mouth. As the dreaded orb came closer it seemed to increase in size; the boy felt as though it now filled his entire field of vision. This swelling object might overwhelm him at any moment, cover his face like a mask emitting pure oxygen to render him lightheaded or unconscious. Beneath the tough surface membrane there was granulation; it resembled the speckled shell of a grouse egg. Did an embryo lie within? Julius remembered his terrible guilt at collecting and 'blowing' wild birds' eggs. Once hollow, they were labelled and placed on cotton wool in a cardboard box. Julius did not want to peer into this strangely familiar yet alien form, he simply wanted to escape. In order to seek the sanctuary of his parents' bedroom, which adjoined his own, he had to enter the landing area before immediately turning left. Julius had to regain control of his body and move towards the monster he feared. At the last possible moment, or so it seemed at the time, he slid out of bed and ran from his room, momentarily finding himself in closer proximity to the object from the wood. Hyperventilating and nauseous, he had fled the thing which had come to suffocate, infect, or possess him. He told his parents that he had simply had a nightmare and wanted to sleep on the floor in their room for the remainder of the night.

Julius felt that he had suffered a 'near-death' experience, as though he had been rescued from unconsciousness which could have been perpetual. Admittedly, his brain had remained active whilst his body had ceased to function, or had his brain cells continued to generate thoughts and actions whilst he slept? Had the whole sequence been only an hallucination which had occurred during shutdown?

Julius was certain that the *floatershell* had an independent existence; he had not conjured it up from within his own mind. Visible to the naked eye in the outdoors, it had now assumed an indoor presence. Julius meditated on its increased energy; it was becoming more powerful. It had a purpose which he did not yet understand. Perhaps, oh horror, it was a viewing device? It had looked at him from afar, then some years later entered his home. Where would it next locate itself?

Julius was now certain that he was being shadowed. As he grew older he could expect more sightings and increased 'hauntings'. Like Peter Quint in *The Turn of the Screw*, the threat would increase with the passage of time. Quint, the tempter, had begun by first being glimpsed far off, seen in places of danger like the high tower at Bly. Then he had gradually moved closer, looking in at the window, staring up from the garden and finally entering the house where he had beguiled and dominated the boy, Miles, his former companion in life.

It was possible, thought Julius, that this shell which observed and shadowed him, was intending to seduce and parasitize him, like a virus entering the host body. Having infected him, it might live in symbiosis or gradually weaken him and await his dissolution. Julius thought that the embryo within the shell might enter his human DNA and somehow partake in biological evolution, or, having killed him, it might itself undergo reincarnation. After all, life on earth is the product of mutations, thought Julius. But Julius' greatest fear was not death, but possession through the eyes.

In 1978 Julius, now a young man and qualified doctor, had started his specialist training in ophthalmology. He had received no further visits from the orb, but his floaters had become much larger and numerous, especially in the left eye. However, Julius had become increasingly detached from these 'worms and webs', as he called them, and his fear had regressed. Medicine suited him; it nurtured his intellect and satisfied his need to be in control, albeit with deep humanitarian instincts. The psychotic fears of the past had gradually shrunk away. The 1970s were a great era of freedom and increased fun.

Now that he no longer felt besieged by perhaps fallible memories, anticipation and dread, he was free to embark on his beloved experimental work. Almost all his time would be committed to the study of human perception. The eyes were the route to understanding the brain and perhaps achieving immortality. He was still haunted by the glazed eyes of those tiny, beautiful birds that had died in his gentle hands. He still wanted to hold a vulnerable creature and tenderly say: 'He lives.' This longing to return the dead to the living world had been there since his infancy. Indeed, he knew that its origins went back to the accidental death of an orphaned baby hedgehog that he had adopted. Despite his tender care and protection of the delightful, snuffling bundle of soft spikes, Julius' selfishness and carelessness had been the cause of the animal's early death. Julius still blamed himself and mourned the loss. He had never come to terms with his thoughtless behaviour or expiated his guilt. Because he had insisted on taking his tiny 'friend' with him for a bicycle ride, securing him in the front basket, the ensuing damage to the hedgehog was solely his fault. He had never forgotten the terrible sensation of his bicycle wheel as it touched the resistant spikes of the vulnerable animal. Julius had been so lost in the enchantment of the surrounding countryside that day that he had failed to notice 'Perky' escaping from the basket and slipping to the ground. Julius' wheel had run over a back leg. The dear creature seemed to be only slightly injured, but died a few hours later, possibly from shock. The boy wrapped the body in straw and placed it in an old 'National Dried Milk' tin left over from his baby days. He then dug a deep hole beneath a favourite tree in the garden, and buried his little friend. Julius hoped that the burial resembled hedgehog hibernation, and that somehow the tiny animal would return to him next spring. He consoled himself with this fantasy, even though his boundless sense of well-deserved guilt would not really allow him to be comforted. He must suffer for his actions. Never again did Julius take an animal from the wild; he did not trust his own motivation. In the past he had tried to help injured birds, diseased rabbits and the cruelly hunted fox, but thereon, although his love for these animals was even greater, he did not intervene. He owed this principle to his harmless, helpless, spiky friend from the past; he had been a part of Julius' beloved miniature world where the creator took control.

As a young doctor, Julius speculated about the possibly fluid borders between the living and the dead. Was there some pearl-grey zone, or porous membrane through which one might travel? Julius liked to reflect on the possibility of crossing boundaries. After all, it was so easy to retrieve people from the past, simply through an emotional identification and empathy with them. He himself felt unbelievably close to Henry James and to Einstein speculating on his beam of light. At the core of every intensity it seems that time stands still, whether in music, literature, science or maths. Julius was fully aware that in a state of ecstasy, chemical changes in the brain took place and the body was flooded with endorphins.

The mysterious relationship between vision and consciousness enthralled Dr Julius Kandel. He wanted to understand more about the way in which the brain processes incoming data from the sense organs, especially the eyes. What we see through the world's most important lens must be mixed up with the internally generated perceptions of the observer's brain, thought Julius. The storage potential of the brain is so huge, that the number of possible connections between neurons exceeds the number of elementary particles in the universe, so we have excess capacity way beyond the needs of our lifetime. The electrical signals across the brain travel at the speed of light because electrical discharges travel at the speed of light. The human brain is the most complex form of matter in the universe, and a very large area of this organ is devoted to analyzing the visual input stream.

As his middle-years approached, Julius looked back on his 'decade of the human brain', studying the connections between visual circuitry in the cerebral cortex and the retina of the eye. He had related all his findings to the meaning of his own version of reality, a personal universe. He was now convinced that his brain possessed duality; a hidden intruder was living inside his mind in mostly peaceful co-existence. All human brains have two cerebral hemispheres, connected by a large nerve bundle called the corpus callosum, but his other self had decided to become visible to him in a forever flowing, pearl-grey haze or transparent shapes which used his sensory apparatus. In other words, somebody else was viewing him, but also looking out of his eyes.

Another self in the brain explained his occasional fearful visions and also his auditory hallucinations, the nocturnal voice in the head. The voice always had a precise location; he could feel its gentle breath on his ear just before it spoke. The voice never deviated from a single word message such as 'trust', 'now', 'come', or sometimes just his name 'Julius' would be spoken in resonant masculine tones. He wondered if this disembodied voice was urging him to action, an external, even divine voice of motivation. The explanation for this dialectic could be fathomed in many different ways, but he felt convinced that although it was the same voice at each visit, it communicated on behalf of many different people across space and time. On the most recent occasion Julius had simply known immediately that the beatified Cardinal John Henry Newman had spoken to him just before dawn. After the brief encounter he had felt utterly serene and blessed. His neurological pathways and psychology formed a peaceful entity, in intimate harmony with the physical universe. Cardinal Newman had been one of the earliest Christian supporters of Darwin's theory of evolution: 'It does not seem to me to follow that creation is denied because the Creator, millions of years ago, gave laws to matter.'

Julius liked being spoken to by this friend in the shadows of darkness. Surely this massive discharge of electricity crossing his synapses and travelling at the speed of light, took his own consciousness itself 'out of time'. As Einstein had proved, at the speed of light, time would cease to exist. Perhaps Julius was connected in some way to a presence which had itself fallen out of time and space? The past, present and future had become one, just as they were during a psychotic experience. The three temporal levels ceased to exist during this trance like ecstasy; he had been given a perception of the truth and the visual key to the eternal.

The painful and horrifying memory of his third encounter with the *floatershell* in 1966, this time accelerating towards him on the railway track, assumed a newly resolved meaning. The spinning energy ball, which had first been sighted far away, was now growing larger and coming closer to him. Julius' adolescent eyes, now at their full adult size, were inhabited by the sentient floaters seeking to correspond with their enfolded counterpart. Little wonder that Julius had felt infected by the sense of being followed or shadowed. Unlike the nocturnal voice, the filled membrane in the woodland clearing, at the top of the stairs, on the railway line, and through the bedroom window, had never seemed benign. It was always a sudden and unexpected phantom which left Julius trembling and dreading any return.

But he knew at last that he had been chosen to receive this knowledge of higher biological evolution. He could not excrete this 'thing' which possessed him. If necessary, he would have to await his own dissolution at death, when the atoms that made up his body would begin to compose other life-forms or possibly re-group so that he could re-occupy the same place and time. He had frequently been amazed by the coincidences in his life; the word meant 'to occupy the same place or time'. The physical world and the human being were interchangeable, but the possibly immortal human soul evolved in the same way as an animal species. The Gnostic Gospel of Thomas gives these words to Jesus: 'Two will rest in a bed, but one shall die and another will live.' And as Peter Ackroyd has pointed out, English ghosts are alarming but also consoling, because they give some confirmation of an alternative world.

Julius had always identified with the night and nocturnal animals, and even when his specialist ophthalmology training was completed, his passion for understanding the nocturnal eye was obsessional. Cats had always played a very important part in his life; many childhood memories centred on them and he now had four feline companions to share his adult life. All his cats, two males and two females, had been rescued by Cats Protection, Julius' favourite charity to which he was devoted.

The most remarkable and beautiful feature of the eye of a cat, thought Julius, is the *tapetum lucidum*, meaning 'bright carpet'. Composed of a thick reflective membrane, it is an adaption for night vision. When the light is re-emitted back to the retina, the cat's eyes appear to glow. The tapetum lining the back of the eye acts like a mirror so that the light actually passes through the lens from the back of the eye and shines through the pupil, allowing us to see the glorious 'bright carpet'. Julius identified with the glowing eyes of the predator, and also loved their claws, teeth, sounds, and acute sense of smell. Nocturnal hunters like the cat and the owl aroused feelings of fear and awe in Julius.

He pondered on the strangeness of the mystical number three which is so significant in analysing the structure of the eye. Basically, the not-entirely-spherical eye is made up of three coats, enclosing three transparent structures. Of the three coats the outermost layer is composed of the cornea and sclera, the middle layer of choroid, ciliary body and iris, and the innermost, of the retina, which can be seen with an ophthalmoscope. Within these three coats are three transparent bodies, the aqueous humour, vitreous jelly and the flexible lens, all connected via the pupil whose size is regulated by the iris. The pupil of the eye is its aperture, the iris is the diaphragm that serves as the aperture stop.

Julius became totally absorbed in the examination of the human eye. To know someone properly one must look at their retina which would release its secrets to him. This was the moment of revelation and insight into the purpose of the hauntings which had encircled his life. As soon as the eye moves it adjusts its exposure both chemically and geometrically. Initial dark adaption takes place in approximately four seconds of profound, unchanging darkness.

Full adaption through changes in retinal chemistry takes thirty minutes. Julius had been interested to observe the precautions employed to protect the Chilean miners, newly released from their 'Hades' deep within the earth. They had all been given expensive wraparound sunglasses in preparation for their return to the world of light. The men would need to wear these protective shields for many days following their rescue from the mine.

The eye itself is an astounding optical instrument, but it is much more than a sublime version of a camera. Only 10 percent of vision comes from the specific visual centres in the human brain, the remainder is dispersed throughout the brain. Thus what we perceive is partly an internally generated version of reality, and because our brains have such enormous data storage capacity, it is possible that inside our heads are vast libraries. Julius' early mental enrichment had left him with a feeling of separation from the uncertain realities of the external world. We perceive what our minds dictate as being necessary to our evolutionary survival, was the view of many scientists. 'The perceiver and the perceived are but two aspects of one unity,' said David Bohm. At times Julius felt that his brain was really a gigantic lens.

The new scientific belief insists that all our senses interconnect in a highly complex way. Modern research, especially through brain-scanning techniques, is concentrating on the psychology and physiology of perception through all our senses. Studies indicate that through neuroplasticity, cortical re-mapping areas of the brain are far more versatile and interconnected than was previously thought. The brain is able to anticipate and choose what it will see up to 20 seconds in advance. In this way it is able to give meaning and shape to an overwhelming input of random information. This process of selection is essential to human survival in our complex world. One area of investigation has been of a 'human bat', a blind man who, when cycling, uses echo location to 'see'. A brain scan revealed that the blind cyclist was employing his visual cortex in the process of echo location; the visual area of his brain was processing sound as vision – the brain of the 'batman' was seeing through sound.

Julius was captivated by this 2010 story of human echo location. He was convinced that the purpose of his long-ago encounters with the *floatershell* and the voice in darkness was to reconnect with that eternal echo which spoke of our duality and ultimate complete resurrection. His vitreous opacities and manifest ghostly encounters had revealed to him alone the visible infinite filaments, of which the flocculi on the surface of the sun were mere traces.

'Light and darkness, life and death,
Right and left, are inseparable twins.

For the good are not wholly good
Nor the wicked wholly wicked,
Nor is life merely life,
Nor death merely death;
Each will return to its primal source.

But those who transcend these apparent opposites are eternal.'

The Gnostic Gospel of Philip

The Bridge

Black obsidian mirror

'Above it stood the Seraphims: each one had six wings; with twain he covered his face, and with twain he covered his feet, and with twain he did fly.' (Isaiah 6: 2-3)

Many tragic moments are now endlessly replayable. A real event is perhaps imagined, changed and re-imagined from a slightly altered perspective, but as if it were taking place over and over again. A specific act of abduction, abandonment, or death is viewed again and again, open to interpretation by the observer. Imagine Theseus leaving the deserted Ariadne on the shore of Naxos, or the intensity of the moment when Bacchus sees Ariadne, 'god and girl pause on a single heartbeat'. Or think of Actaeon's forbidden gaze at the naked Diana bathing in her cavern pool: love and death instantly juxtaposed: seen through the eyes of Titian. These events are unchanging, only the colours of the old master fading and darkening with time to become an ever-more beautiful masterpiece. Not so the modern tragedy, the frozen moment captured on video camera, paused and re-run, robbed of the dignity which the ancient Greeks thought of as life and fate.

In April 2006, a writer, on holiday, was the anonymous witness to a tragedy on the Humber Bridge, which CCTV also captured and subsequently beamed into millions of homes, allowing all to participate and speculate.

The writer, a respected creator of literary fiction, had visited the Hull area with his teenage children to see the marine life at *The Deep*, and subsequently explore the Lincolnshire Wolds. But he also wanted to visit Britain's largest suspension bridge; the main character in his current novel was obsessed by bridge disasters and their symbolic meaning. For him, the bridge was about strength and masculinity; he was as interested in their construction as in their destruction, but he knew in his heart that the origins of this strange preoccupation lay in his own childhood. At primary school he had always been academically outstanding, but he was also known to dream and lose concentration. He preferred to withdraw into a world of his own where *he* was its interpreter. At the age of seven he had been enjoying a history lesson on Horatio, famously holding up the bridge, when the teacher suggested that the entire class spend the remaining 30 minutes writing an illustrated story on the hero and his feat. Our infant writer was enthralled and became immersed in his task, drawing with great care and adding lots of detail. He felt proud but unsurprised when the teacher chose him to tell *his* story to the class and hold up his picture for all to see. He stood up to read with confidence, but feeling especially proud of his drawing, decided to show it to everyone before they listened to his account of the Roman hero. At first, as he rotated with the opened book, there was complete silence, but then smirking faces and squeals of laugher surrounded him. He looked anxiously at his teacher; she too was laughing at him. When he sat down Mrs Dickon explained that he had misinterpreted the phrase 'holding up the bridge'. Horatio had defended the bridge with all his courage and strength, but he had not been underneath it literally supporting it from beneath with his great arms held aloft like Samson! All was ruined for the small boy, never again would he show his work to anyone or trust anyone in authority. Instead of pursuing a career in academia, he continued with his literary fiction and occasional editing work.

The writer and his two sons, Louis and Max, had loved their Easter holiday trip to *The Deep*, Hull's new marine spectacular. The boys had been particularly fascinated by the sharks, seeing their underwater beauty and grace as supreme predators. They had wanted to go into the tank and swim with them, but there had not been time to do so on one of the organised dives available to the public. Having at last persuaded Louis and Max to leave the exhilarating marina, he had promised them a visit to the huge bridge, elegantly spanning the turbulent waters below.

Tomorrow they would travel onwards to Lincoln. The writer wished to re-visit his beloved golden cathedral, with its unique Easter sepulchre depicting the sleeping Roman soldiers, guarding Christ's tomb. The urge to wander, the freedom of being on the road had been with him since childhood when he had run wild in the countryside. He identified with the poet John Clare, finding solace in the journey, but also seeking home. Clare's poignant glimpse of the gypsies, after he has escaped the asylum, always reminded the writer of his own friendship with a gypsy at the age of eight or nine – a very impressionable time when experiences leave a lifelong mark.

His closest friend, Harry, had certainly remained with him in spirit. As he drove towards the great bridge, with the children singing in the rear of the car, the writer thought back to his first meeting with the unique Harry Agus, always known at school as 'Hagus'. The boy had arrived suddenly, out of the blue, dressed shabbily in an old suit, jacket and short trousers, clearly cut down from his father's clothes. The other children laughed at his olive complexion, and black curly hair. Despite this mockery, Harry smiled affably and invited the other children to share his knowledge of animals and the countryside. But I, alone, was invited to his caravan, to meet his parents and the horse. There were also much-loved pets, including cats and dogs, birds and a ferret. The wooden caravan was beautifully decorated inside; it was full of intricate painted designs and lots of copper and brass objects. There were tiny curtains in Harry's small sleeping compartment, and even an indoor stove for heating and cooking. They often ate rabbit, either stewed in the large pot, or roasted on a spit over an outdoor fire. Harry shared all his treasures with me and taught me everything about the countryside, including how to poach from gamekeepers. Looking back on this time, I suppose that Harry would now be looked upon as neglected, and leading a marginal existence. Certainly, his father drank too much and could be harsh, with occasional outbursts of violent temper, but to me Harry's life seemed idyllic. Living in the caravan so close to the natural world, was enthralling, I thought. My own mother started sending food for the numerous dogs and cats. Like me, she identified with outsiders and had no time for convention.

Then, one bright day toward the beginning of the summer holidays, Harry was absent. 'Helping his father,' said our headmistress. The very next day he returned to school with a handmade present for me. It was a picture of a dog, taken from the cover of a chocolate box, and decorated with ribbons. I had seen this photograph many times hanging up by Harry's latticed window; I knew how much Harry loved it. Solemnly, he gave it to me, saying that I must always remember him and have the picture as a keepsake. He had willingly renounced his most precious possession.

Harry's sudden departure was a terrible blow. He had accepted it as an inevitable consequence of the nomadic life of his family; he was accustomed to moving on and did not complain. After many months of sadness and introspection I seemed to recover from the loss of my closest friend but deep inside I was wounded and bleeding. This childhood trauma of separation left me hypersensitive to aloneness. Intimate, lasting friendships were always more important to me than a brief love affair. In any case, the ones I truly loved were my children. My own father had been absent; he had disappeared shortly after my birth.

Both the chronology and topography of this holiday with Louis and Max had been chosen carefully. Our visit to the famous toll bridge, followed by Lincoln Cathedral, had to take place at Easter, the time of resurrection. This was my careful choice as background for a future novel; the theme was to be the afterlife, especially of those who have died by their own hand.

I had intended to take the boys for a walk along windswept Spurn Head, but having looked at photographs of this forlorn place, they rejected the idea. Max, in particular, was impatient to get to the bridge and walk across on the pedestrian way. He said that he longed to be suspended in the sky! As I gazed into his beautiful dark eyes I remembered my own childhood dream of flight. I had actually made some crude wings, using the balsa wood and silk from my model aeroplane kits. Having assembled the wings and with great difficulty, tied them onto my back, I shinned up to the garage roof. Although it appeared to be a very long way down to the soft green lawn, I took a run across the roof and jumped off the edge. I flapped the flimsy wings but there was neither lift nor control. Falling like a stone, I crash-landed on the empty paddling pool; it cracked under my weight. The wings were useless; I decided to hang them up for a while.

Within almost every human being there is the desire for flight. Leonardo's angels have realistic bird wings; I could look forever at his Gabriel in *The Annunciation*. As children we all want to fly with Peter Pan, to travel where and when we please. And this earthly longing seems to transfer to detailed imagining of the afterlife. A singer friend, whose wife died several years ago, claims to be in daily touch with her through divining rods. She has told him it is now possible for her to fly at will, anywhere she chooses. He has also told me that, like the angels in mediaeval art, the dead Elizabeth hovers just above him at about ceiling height.

Musing on these supernatural events, I approached the graceful and elegant bridge, my sons running eagerly ahead towards the foot access. Suddenly, they halted and knelt down to examine some object on the ground which I could not identify from my distant vantage point. I could see that they were laughing and teasing each other, so it occurred to me that they had probably found a used condom, discarded perhaps by a couple who had enjoyed a sexual union over water. As children we frequently dream of endlessly and tirelessly swimming like Tom, the little chimney-sweep in *The Waterbabies*, or running vast distances, like Homer's Achilles, the 'swift-footed son of Peleus'.

As I gazed into the distance, beyond the kneeling boys, I noticed two small, blurred figures dressed in black. They seemed to be very close to the edge of the bridge, holding hands and facing east. Suddenly, one of the figures appeared to jump freely from the great bridge into the swirling waters beneath. Horrified, I continued to watch the remaining figure. Time stood still. I felt unable to move and my ears buzzed.

Another sudden movement, and the second figure disappeared. In the space of only moments, two people had ended their lives.

Fortunately, my two sons had been so preoccupied with their find that they had not witnessed the suicides. Calling, and beckoning to them, I bundled them, without explanation, into the car and drove off as quickly as possible. I did not want to become personally involved in these dreadful events, and in any case I already had what I wanted. I had a story to tell, and luckily already knew the ending.

Shortly after the writer had fled the double suicide, the obsessive media coverage had begun, greatly assisted by CCTV pictures of the event:

Death Plunge Mother and Son Caught On CCTV

'Facing east, but dressed in black, the two small, blurred figures were seen to jump from the great bridge, soon disappearing in the turbulent waters beneath.'

At first, the dramatic headlines gave only brief details of the known facts, but newspaper accounts soon metamorphosed into speculation. There were many interpreters of the mother and son death plunge, and the wider family of the deceased were interviewed by reporters as well as by the police. Overall, it was concluded that the chronology and topography for the suicides had been carefully selected. Kingston upon Hull was redolent with happy memories for mother and son, described as 'soul-mates' – prefiguring their tragic departure from life. Because the boy, Ryan, loved trains, they had travelled by train to the suicide location. Two previous suicide attempts were documented, the first by jumping off Beachy Head, and the second by walking into the sea – death by drowning.

The boy (Ryan), was known to suffer from *fragile X syndrome*, a learning disability linked to autism. The CCTV footage showed that mother and son were dressed in the colour of mourning. There was no father figure in Ryan's life, he had disappeared early on. The mother and child relied wholly on a support group of women, mainly Ryan's adoring grandmother and aunts.

Alison Davies (the boy's mother) had journeyed with her autistic son, on the Stockport Express, arriving at Paragon Station in Hull. Police believe that they took a taxi from the station to the bridge. Both dressed in black and holding hands, they were seen exiting the ticket barriers and leaving the city's Paragon Station, Alison intent on their plunge into the icy waters of the river.

The body of Ryan, aged 12, was not found until April 17th 2006; he was located 20 miles from the site of his death leap. Alison's body had been found much closer to the bridge, and within a few days of her suicide. The newspapers blamed the tragedy on society, on the indifference of society. This was the predictable and simplistic interpretation typical of the print media, both local and national: 'The deaths of Alison Davies and her autistic son, Ryan, highlight the tragedy of maternal depression...the dark side of mothering.' (Debbie Taylor, *The Sunday Times*, April 23, 2006)

However, the sisters of Alison Davies, were reported in *The Sunday Times* of May 21st 2006, as viewing her fatal jump off the Humber Bridge with her beloved son Ryan as 'a selfless act to end their torment'. Adored within his family, Ryan had been isolated and bullied at school. In the wider world, beyond home, he was a lonely outsider, an outcast. He loved football, but the other boys would not play with him when he became an exceptionally strong, large, and unpredictable 12-year-old. His life was to be a long childhood of increasing withdrawal and frustration.

The act of suicide can take many forms, but whether it is by hurling oneself over a precipice, a bullet in the brain, hanging or drowning – its underlying cause is the black-dog depression. My Great-Aunt Evelyn, the mother of two daughters, aged eight and five, threw herself into the fast-moving waters of the River Derwent. As a little girl, Evelyn had been adopted by a lady whose surname was Ratcliffe. This person was very Victorian in manner and appearance; she already had several daughters and one son, but arranged to adopt Evelyn from a nearby convent. Mrs Ratcliffe adored George Francis Holmes, her only son, but had little time for her female offspring. George was her darling boy, but had married a woman of whom she disapproved, and Evelyn had also chosen unwisely, thought her adoptive mother. By the time World War II was raging, Evelyn already had two young girls to care for, whilst her husband, Arthur, was philandering in the army. Rumours of his infidelity reached her and he was also drinking heavily. Evelyn complained that when he came home on leave all he wanted her for was to 'make babies'. Soon, she was pregnant with an unwanted third child, and despite being very religious, tried to terminate the pregnancy herself. Having succeeded in inducing a miscarriage, she was stricken with guilt and despair, becoming more and more withdrawn.

She was living with Ivy and Horace, her sister and brother-in-law. They were very kind and tried to provide a home for their distressed sister with the lovely children and irresponsible, selfish husband. He rarely sent any money to support his family.

One night, when she and her daughters were asleep, Evelyn decided that the end had come: she could continue no longer. During the night she climbed out of the bedroom window, waking her five-year-old daughter Kathy. The small child, sleepy, but seeing her mother unlatching the window, asked her, 'What are you doing, Mummy?' Evelyn told her to go back to sleep, and taking her handbag and coat, walked towards the river. When Ivy came in the next morning with Evelyn's cup of tea, she felt absolute shock at Evelyn's absence. The police and dogs were used to search, but all they found were her handbag and a few personal items on the river bed. A psychic was called in by the family. She walked straight over to the window, crying and saying, 'Oh, I am so sorry, she is gone but she will be found. She is lying in very deep water and wants you to pray for her to be forgiven. The moment the waters closed over her, she longed to get back to her children'. Evelyn's daughter, Margaret, was subsequently taken in by close relatives, but young Kathy remained with Ivy and Horace. So, tragically, the bereft sisters were separated and their father remained estranged until their adulthood. They always blamed him for the death of their mother, for his indifference to her turmoil.

Writing of Mostar Bridge, after the Bosnian War, Dan Cruickshank meditates on its reconstruction:

'But, I wonder, is it nothing other than a comely mask hiding a bitter and distorted grimace, a scarred visage, a scream of rage? You can rebuild a bridge, but you can't, I fear, so easily repair a shattered soul or a broken heart'.

The details of the double suicide of Alison and Ryan kept changing, as media reports altered their emphasis. *The Guardian* account on Wednesday April 19th 2006, exactly one week after the tragic leap, described 'A mother and son smiling at the station. Then two specks on the edge of a bridge.' The grainy figures were described as 'ant-like', clambering over a security railing on the eastern footpath of the Humber Bridge. Moments later one is seen falling towards the waters 100 feet below. Eight seconds pass, then the other figure falls too. Police specialists had 30 seconds of poor-quality footage, which they were attempting to enhance, taken by a camera high up on one of the bridge's twin towers. Police said that it was very difficult to ascertain which of the two people had been the first to jump, the footage from the Paragon railway station at Hull shows Mrs Davies and 12-year-old Ryan arriving in the city earlier, apparently cheerful and chatting to one another. Under the care of his mother, the boy had developed into a cheerful footballer who was popular with others and also enjoyed 'doing wheelies on his bike'.

Ryan's body was washed 10 miles upstream by strong and variable tidal movements; pathologists carried out tests for drugs or painkillers which might have been administered to him. Detective Superintendent Colin Andrews confirmed that Alison Davies had left a despairing note after leaving her mother's home in Marple, near Stockport, the day before the suicide jump. The note expressed her depression and belief that she had failed as a mother to Ryan. Mrs Davies made it clear in her note that the plan was 'to end the pain'. The CCTV images showed that there was no sign of a struggle on the bridge. 'If the images are of Ryan and Alison, then Ryan was not forcibly dragged anywhere and there was no violence between them,' said Mr Andrews.

The crackly and interrupted mobile phone message from the bridge asked for police to tell the woman caller's mother that there was no more need to worry. The line went dead before she could give any names, so police took no further action at this stage. Minutes later, mother and son clambered over the eastern side of the bridge, facing Hull where Alison and Ryan had spent a happy period some years before, and plunged to their deaths in sinister black depths of the Humber.

'*Austistic Awareness*' campaigners, and experts on maternal depression immediately blamed the double tragedy on under-funding by local councils who had failed to provide adequate respite care for families with autistic members. Lindsay Cook, a sister of Alison Davies, endorsed this viewpoint, saying, 'We would like to highlight the ongoing plight of families coping with mental health and learning disabilities issues in order to spare other families from experiencing this pain.'

However, the overall verdict by the sisters was that Alison Davies' fatal jump off the Humber Bridge with her son Ryan was a selfless act to end their torment: 'A mother's leap of love.' Ryan had been the focus of Alison's life. In her suicide note, left in the kitchen, and found the next day by her brother-in-law Andy Cook, she wrote that she didn't want Ryan to be lonely any more. In her 999 call just before she jumped telling her mother not to worry, she said: 'Everything will be all right.' Her sister, Lindsay Cook, said of Alison's final leap, 'It was the ultimate sacrifice … How brave is that?' According to the family, Alison was in complete control of events on the bridge, where she and Ryan spent a calm and playful 40 minutes before they slipped out of sight. After the double funeral in Hull, Alison's mother and grandmother to Ryan, said: 'I'm sad for myself but I am glad they are safe and peaceful at last, and together.'

Alison was a carrier of *fragile X syndrome (FXS)*, the condition associated with autism and learning difficulties, which Ryan had inherited. It is passed from mother to son, and research suggests that carrier mothers are themselves prone to depression. Ryan was inconsolable as a baby and the family feared he might be blind or deaf. Later, he attended mainstream school, but most of his lessons were taken in the special needs unit.

Her sisters wish to highlight the disease so that Alison has not died in vain, but they do not blame social services for her death. Her sister, Julie Armand, emphasised that Alison was an independent, proud and private woman: 'I don't want her to be remembered just as "the woman on the bridge" … she had a deep abiding and consuming love for Ryan.'

Alison had been artistic and creative, with a great love of fashion. She owned many silk party dresses and 'strappy' dancing shoes, but with no opportunities to enjoy wearing them. The invitations never came and hers was a solitary existence. As Ryan grew in size and strength he became very difficult to control, and Alison's family began to talk of residential care for him. His mother had recently passed her driving test and exams needed to be a medical secretary; a new job awaited her. But the thought of committing Ryan to the primary care of others tortured and troubled her; she felt profound guilt. Nevertheless, the home had become a battleground with her difficult son; it was hard to keep him safe. Even though other children his own age teased him mercilessly for his retarded language, he wanted to play with them. His school reports were growing worse, whilst at home he would run wild and escape on his bike. His mother could no longer protect him from the outside world, and felt that there was no positive future for either of them: hence their suicide pact.

Mr Andrews, of Humberside Police, referring to the contents of Alison's suicide-note said: 'Clearly she felt a burden and clearly she felt that she wanted to relieve her family of that burden. And she strongly indicated she intended to travel to the Humber Bridge to harm herself and Ryan. Eight seconds separated the two falls, but it was very difficult to say which of the persons went first. Alison had suffered from depression since the age of 16; her depression was said to switch on and off with no apparent reason, making it very hard to handle.'

Alison's best friend, Tracy Hinds, interpreted the suicide as a positive act through which Ryan and his mother could at last be together, 'as she would have wanted'. The public in general saw their last tragic journey as an indictment of so-called 'care in the community'. Morene Conway of London wrote: 'What sadness and torment those two human beings must have suffered. Finally a bureaucratic response from some distant response centre. Care in the community? What care?!'

Liliana's account

Paying grave attention to all these newspaper headlines, and the endlessly repeated video footage of the two small, blurred figures seen to jump from the great bridge, was Liliana – the sweet and clever little daughter of Blaise Vyner. She had been named for the lily held by Gabriel the messenger, and given to Mary at the annunciation. Leonardo's twilight depiction of this event within a decorated walled garden bordered by cypress trees, was her mother's favourite painting. She simply loved the atmosphere of the tender, yet reverent, encounter, full of possibilities. Although only five years of age, Liliana had a precocious reading facility and outstripped all her peer group in this respect. Soon she would be starting school and Liliana looked forward to that day with anxious intensity. It should be the beginning of an exciting new journey, but difficulties in pre-school had made Liliana fear that the experience might fail to thwart her doom. She believed overwhelmingly in fate, and utterly rejected the fateless. The two could not be reconciled.

Like the hazy figures in the CCTV footage, she and her mother were said to enjoy a symbiotic relationship. They usually walked together hand in hand; their contact was intense, intimate but relaxed. They did not oppress one another; they remained free. But Liliana knew that in reality, like the two people featured in Goya's painting of Dr Arietta and his patient, 'the one so desperate and the other so consoling', she and her mother were to become the living embodiment of an ancient Greek tragedy.

Liliana remembered the blissful stillness of all those days alone with her mother, the warm, comforting sensation of her cheek against the carpet as she listened to a story. But the time had now come to put on her uniform and be attentive to teachers and new friends. Liliana liked her smart, brown hat encircled by an orange ribbon bearing the school crest. Her soft brown woollen blazer was piped with the same orange satin, and her scarf and tie had the same wonderful orange stripes: like the tiger, she was magnificently marked.

On the first day of school, Liliana's mother adjusted her daughter's tie, and holding her in both arms fondly kissed the warm cheeks, saying, 'Goodbye, darling, I'll collect you at

3.30.' Liliana pulled up her socks and gave a final tug to the overly long satchel strap, before rushing across the playground and into the heavenly rose-coloured porch of the ancient school entrance.

On that first day her sense of foreboding departed, to be replaced by a sunlit drowsy sense of contentment and concealment. She felt tranquil but impenetrable, in control, like Alice in Wonderland. She liked the formality and conformity fostered by the strictly apportioned hours of the school day. Rigid routine suited her changeable, melancholy nature; she had been described by her absent father as 'like an opal'.

As the term passed, Liliana's idiosyncrasies were almost obliterated by the highly educated and beautifully spoken headmistress Miss Alexandre Winbolt. This was the opposite of life at home. Liliana felt that her headmistress might rescue her from the fate which otherwise awaited. The world of school offered the only possibility of escape; it was highly unlikely that her mother would die relatively young, and thus set her free from such an intense bond.

Nevertheless, this idyllic new life had its moments of despair. This arena of torment was the playground where the other children excluded her from their games. She knew that she was exceptional and thus incurred jealousy, but, despite enjoying her otherness, Liliana wanted to be included and have a 'best friend'. Her saviour proved to be the skipping rope; it was she who introduced this simple toy as a lunchtime diversion. It offered both solitary pleasure for the rejected individual, but also the opportunity for cooperation in shared games. With a skipping rope one never felt alone, and it disguised solitariness from onlookers. Liliana quickly became the knowledgeable, sought-after leader, followed and admired by girls and boys alike. Her schoolfellows were attentive to her ideas for skipping games and listened to her words. She was full of suggestions for ever more complicated solo and team games involving the skipping rope. After only a few weeks everyone at school had acquired one, and even the older children deferred to her skill and imagination.

Fortunately, this new love endured, and often at playtime she was borne aloft by her crowd of excited classmates. They encouraged her to show off and become competitive. This precious link to others, brought about by her idea of skipping, transformed her primary school years into something profoundly joyous. Protected by outward confidence and popularity, her inmost self was able to become ever more beautiful and complex.

These formative years were never to be forgotten; she was certain of that. They had ultimately banished her deep-rooted anguish. She could see the future now, with breathtaking clarity. It was as if a mirror of divination revealed all; she became Doctor Dee looking into the depths of his obsidian mirror. Liliana saw angels and devils, the souls of the living and the dead. Most of all she looked into the beautiful face of a boy named Michael, remembered always. He had soft, curly, black hair, olive skin and wonderful dark-blue eyes. His handsome gypsy looks were illuminated by a compassionate, sensitive nature. He was surrounded by animals, which he cared for with great tenderness. He reminded Liliana of Leonardo da Vinci, and she saw that he was able to fly. She would go with him: two heavenly beings.

* * *

The desire for flight or any kind of effortless movement lies deep within us. As children we frequently dream of flying like Peter Pan, or endlessly and tirelessly swimming like Tom in *The Water Babies*, or running forever like Homer's Achilles, the swift-footed son of Peleus.

Some people believe that in the afterlife we are able to fly, going wherever we wish almost instantly. Like the angels in mediaeval paintings we hover at ceiling height to be near our loved ones and watch over them. The ancient Greeks developed the concept of the Katascopos, the one who sees from above, and their angels were the Nikes: the majestic Winged Nike of Samothrace evokes both victory and mourning. She is an awe-inspiring paradox of unbelievable beauty, the combination of triumph and tragedy as in the hero Achilles.

As Liliana gazed into the green obsidian mirror, which belonged to her mother, she saw at first a hazy image of the strange boy on the huge bridge. He seemed to be encircled by darkness, as though viewing her from the underworld. As the eerie haze cleared, their eyes met. Liliana was the first to speak:

'Hello, young boy. I recognise you and urgently wish to question you. Is it possible that you might answer my questions?' said Liliana gently but quickly.

The boy responded slowly and seemed to be confused. 'I can talk about the past but not the future,' he said, telling Liliana that he was searching for his mother but could not find her. 'I know that I died first, but she followed me within moments, so why are we now separated?' he asked the image gazing at him in the obsidian blackness. 'Who made the decision to jump from the bridge?' said Liliana, secretly appalled by the fate of the boy and his mother. 'Surely, she should have protected you, not caused you to drown and remain bloated and rotting in the water?' asserted Liliana in horror. The boy answered angrily, refuting the girl's guilt-laden missiles. He said that his mother had gently sent him to fulfil his destiny. There had been no violence, no compulsion. To kill something deeply loved to ensure that no harm befalls it, is an act of love, he argued. 'Are you so sure of her motive?' said Liliana. 'Yes,' said Ryan. 'We were both doomed from the beginning – her depression was a dignified acceptance of the truth – of the cruel world around us – to which neither of us could relate!' 'I thought you had a severe learning disability, or autism or something,' said Liliana, surprised by Ryan's fluency. 'Not anymore,' he replied. 'In my infancy I was a bullied misfit, but because of my loving mother those early years were also magical and protected. We might have withdrawn, but we had our own way of communicating – special to us alone. We didn't seek state-sanctioned help; we knew that it would not provide a solution to our problems.' Liliana was stunned by Ryan's certainty; she felt that she must mention the press and television reports of those events on the bridge. 'But, Ryan,' she interjected, 'What do you think of the outcome from the media coverage of your suicide? Your aunts have said that their dead sister had always suffered from depression, but often failed to take her medication. They said that as you grew older and stronger, she could no longer cope with you. Is this true?'

Ryan remained silent for a very long time. His face in the obsidian mirror began to recede, becoming increasingly opaque. Liliana waited patiently for him to answer, hoping that he would remain with her and not disappear into memory. 'Everyone will say that my mother's decision to jump, taking me with her, was caused by untreated depression. My mother would say that her intention was that we would leave the earth together – she was there at my beginning and my end. People who say that through her actions she murdered me, an innocent child, in an act of selfish destruction might also have a valid point of view. Or did I, like a sinister parasite pull her into my hopelessness and destroy *her*? Even though I remember that she told me to jump first, who really controlled events?' Liliana did not know what to say. Suddenly she wanted to escape this sinister interview and leave the darkness. She felt akin to Orpheus obsessed, failing to retrieve Eurydice from the underworld.

The ancient Greeks say that there is life and then there is fate. Liliana reflected on these distant words, and suspended any judgement on Ryan's account of events on the Humber suspension bridge. She also remembered the Greek concept of *Katascopos*, 'the one who sees from above'. By their dramatic and poignant end in the dark waters beneath the great bridge, the boy and his mother had metamorphosed. They were now immortals, tragic and heroic, and like Achilles, had bathed in 'Myth's river'.

Liliana felt sad but pleased when the boy disappeared, still searching and longing for his mother – a fading image in the green volcanic glass. Would the awkward boy, who had achieved immortality in exchange for his human happiness, be granted the favour of wandering among the dead in search of his mother? 'The entities watching over us from the other side of death' might permit this as the lonely boy was now removed from all earthly attachments.

Liliana gazed into the mirror for the last time. Coming into focus as though returning to existence, was the face of Ryan's dead mother, multiplied to infinity. Love had brought her back, but Liliana knew that she could not comfort her son. Like Orpheus, the boy 'would take with him into immortality only the mask substantiating his memories'.

Angel Blue-eyes and the Golden Shoes

Rapunzel

    She saw herself as *Rapunzel*, the imprisoned fairy-tale princess combing her long golden locks as she awaits rescue from her high tower with neither stairs nor doors. It had been her favourite story as a child. Like *Rapunzel*, her perpetual victimhood would draw forth a man of sensitivity and devotion to impregnate her. In spite of being 'spotted with commonness', to use George Eliot's phrase, she knew exactly how to attract a fine nature and selfless love and use it for her own selfish purpose. There were parallels with the story of Lydgate and Rosamund in *Middlemarch*, she being the basil plant feeding upon a murdered man's brain. The image of parasitism is most apt.

Both the brothers Grimm and George Eliot use natural imagery to great effect. *Rapunzel* is taken by the witch because her mother, when pregnant, craved the plant rampion, and persuaded her husband to steal it from the witch's garden. In exchange for the delicious plant the witch claimed the baby *Rapunzel* with hair as fine as spun gold. In Eliot's novel of provincial life, fair Rosamund builds a fantasy world around Doctor Lydgate. Her egotism directs her towards a dashing and clever outsider. As Rosamund is selfish, narcissistic, shallow and vain she becomes bitter when Lydgate disappoints her. Through marriage she aims to raise her social standing, escape her narrow home to live a comfortable, carefree life elsewhere.

In early infancy Layla had been fought over by her weak father and indifferent mother. Layla's parents had seemed very happy together during the first years of their marriage. Up until their little daughter's fourth birthday, they had lots of fun doting on the tiny child and giving her all that she wanted. She soon learned to ask for more and within a few years of her birth the house overflowed with toys. At Christmas time there was always a giant Santa sack 'For Layla'. She did not seem to be especially intelligent but neither of her parents minded this; they themselves were not very intelligent. Layla's mother always imagined that her daughter's sole ambition would be to have a wonderful wedding; she looked forward to tiaras, veils and golden shoes.

When Layla reached her fourth birthday her father had already been drinking heavily for a couple of years. His arthritic hip had been replaced but the outcome was unsatisfactory, and he was in almost-constant pain. He believed that he was the victim of medical incompetence and complained obsessively about his doctor. The local practice eventually removed him from their list after a series of abusive, irrational incidents had taken place at the surgery.

His descent into sherry, self-pity and life on benefits ended his marriage, but left him with a young daughter to care for. Layla's parents had battled over her during their long process of separation; she remembered the terrible arguments between them and how they had once fought by each holding one of her arms and pulling in opposite directions. Despite a lack of any true maternal feelings for her child, Layla's mother felt pride of possession towards her little daughter, and frustrated loathing and anger towards her discarded husband. She had been involved with other men for some years during the marriage, and in many ways her beloved dog meant far more to her than her child. Also, she had soon realised that it was her husband who took the role of mother and seemed to be far more interested in having a boyfriend than a wife. His homosexual inclinations had developed even further towards the end of Layla's early years, and these barely-disguised same-sex affairs had confirmed the estrangement of his wife. Her contempt for him was increasing.

Layla herself was in conflict. She wanted her parents to stay together and be happy in the worship of their 'little princess', as they always called her. But her survival instincts told her to cling to her father and paternal grandmother, as she was genuinely close to the latter. Layla's mother had grown up in a children's home so had never experienced parental love, whereas her father came from a large extended family of Irish Liverpuddlians. Remaining with her erratic, dysfunctional father would be turbulent, but he would spoil her with endless presents, whilst 'Nan' would provide mother-love and look after her in a practical way.

In her teens, Layla moved into her grandmother's tiny flat in a sheltered housing complex for the elderly. She had often escaped there after rows with her father, who was drinking heavily and constantly complaining about lack of support from Social Services. He had no insight into his dependency problems, but neither did his daughter. They shared a propensity for grandiose schemes intended to confer status and wealth; neither father nor daughter had any awareness of their own limitations. Both were fantasists with an overriding sense of victimhood. Egotistical, insignificant and perpetually aggrieved they sought status through disapproval of almost everything and everyone that they were incapable of understanding. They fed off one another with the oft-repeated phrase 'it's disgusting!' They had no humility, or respect for people of intellect or education, and disapproved of ethnic minorities. 'I'm not having no Muslim having my cat', said Layla when neighbours with a disabled son who enjoyed having the cat on his lap, offered to adopt Layla's neglected, highly affectionate female cat. She was later discarded by Layla, and new kittens were acquired.

Jealous and envious, Layla and her father revelled in the New-Labour-sanctioned opportunities for living off the despised middle-classes whose children were now held captive by the State in the comprehensive schools. Escape was possible at the age of 16 when a selection process at least operated, but it often took several years to recover from the disadvantages of a comprehensive education aimed at the mentality of the majority. Large numbers of cultured and intelligent children did not survive. They either failed to reach their full potential or were destroyed completely by the mob dominating the school.

This system entirely suited the limited aspirations of Layla as she prepared to celebrate her sixteenth birthday. Observing her many cousins who had become teenage single mothers living in the pleasant houses to which they were entitled, she decided that she could 'go one better'. Her scheme for the future would be helped greatly by the current New-Labour demonisation of men, and a Cherie-Blair-style legal system which favoured women. All that was required on her part was plenty of guile, a brief period of hard work, some sexual risk, and the mantle of victimhood. She read the celebrity magazines and tabloid newspapers; everyone loved and sympathised with a female victim especially one with a child. In another five or six years she would have successfully arranged her life as a martyr. All her plebeian circle would admire and pity her blameless self. They would be one chorus, saying, 'It's disgusting'.

Layla was obsessed with the late Diana, Princess of Wales. She had long been her model and inspiration. Layla studied and copied the downcast eyes and shy manner of the devoted mother and rejected wife. She was truly in role, even imitating Diana's alleged bulimia and struggle against anorexia. She believed that she resembled the saintly but misunderstood princess, and wanted to visit the Taj Mahal so that she could be photographed in a pose just like her royal, persecuted heroine.

Layla's academic progress was negligible; the school did not expect her to pass any of her GCSE examinations. She blamed her poor results on the failure of the teaching staff to motivate her, and the distraction of a serious relationship with a boyfriend. It was true that most of her energies were directed towards ensnaring this handsome, charming boy who lacked self-confidence, and was unaware of her long-term plans for his future. Obviously, he would be leaving school to attend the local highly-prestigious sixth-form college, and then after A' levels he would continue on to university. In contrast, she had only passed one GCSE and was lucky to be accepted on a social-care course at her nearby college of further education.

However, by emphasising her disrupted home life and pretending that she had no family to support her, she was able to access numerous concessions and benefits. Her claim to be without family or financial help opened numerous doors for her and proved to be an enormous advantage. She lied very effectively and enjoyed the role of poor, deprived, brave Layla. The family of her boyfriend had never sought or received any state support. Layla looked with contempt at their shabby carpets and old-fashioned television. It was true that they were incredibly kind and generous to her; she was always included on trips to the theatre and ballet. She acknowledged their limitless hospitality and generosity but privately derided it. Nothing they did ever impressed her and their very ordinary car was more than four years old. Even her relatives living in council accommodation were driving new cars.

Layla completely misunderstood the welcome she received at her boyfriend's house. She interpreted it as a special sign of personal favour, which it was not. It had always been open house for the children's friends; some had even stayed for an entire summer vacation. But to Layla this attitude was inexplicable; she put it down to stupidity that could be exploited to her advantage. Such people existed to be used, she thought, and would be easily beguiled with a large 'Santa bag' of gifts at Christmas. She had convinced herself that she was deeply in love with the son of the house, and a true friend of his beautiful, clever sister, four years his senior. The whole family were far too high-minded and courteous to guess at or judge her private agenda, although she had to admit that the mother was frighteningly perceptive.

Layla's dream was to follow her boyfriend to university and then play a waiting game until, towards the end of their final year, she would impale him with her pregnancy. Nowadays, everything was loaded in her favour; all she had to do was fantasise. Coming from what the authorities saw as an educationally disadvantaged background, she was allowed much lower entrance requirements. Also, she pretended that the estrangement from her entire family was complete, so a family contribution to financial support would be impossible. This fabrication also ensured that she was given a small council house, which remained hers throughout the entire time at university. Even when her grandmother and father died, she could still have lived at her mother's house, but, instead, claimed that she had no contact with her mother.

With one A' level at the lowest grade and a diploma in an unrelated subject, she managed to gain supported entry to an education degree. Throughout her three unproductive years at university she fell seriously behind and missed most lectures, but was able to use illness as an excuse. Anaemia and bulimia were helpful tools when the education department became suspicious and critical. In all of this self-created chaos she involved her hardworking boyfriend, making him feel responsible for her. He trusted and believed in her; this was his fatal mistake and flaw.

Rather than writing essays, Layla spent most of her student days on eBay, or looking in her favourite shoe-shop *Faith*. She was absolutely obsessed by shoes, especially ones made of gold leather. Layla shopped compulsively, and then took everything back. The clothes she bought were worn once or twice, and then abandoned, like her endless trail of discarded cats. The golden shoes were an exception. Like her longing for a golden-haired child, the shoes became a fetish. When she deliberately stopped taking the contraceptive pill and said that she 'fell pregnant', nobody believed her. To her great disappointment the baby was male. She had always imagined a golden-girl, her own little princess.

To her horror, she suddenly found that she was no longer in control. Her boyfriend had been completely honest and said months before that after university they should go their separate ways. They had continued to have occasional sex because she had told him that she was dying of a rare liver disease which made her infertile. She had carefully documented visits to the liver specialist with her colluding mother, when in fact she had been out shopping. Later on, she invented appointments at a mental-health clinic and gynaecologist.

The astute sister saw exactly what Layla was doing to her beloved brother, and how he was being ruthlessly used. She warned him but it was too late. Layla's hysteria and depression when her grandmother had died had ensured his loyal concern, just as it had when her father died from cirrhosis of the liver. He had been so sweet to her even though she now irritated him and he had completely outgrown his teenage infatuation. It had taken him years to recover from the disastrous social environment of a comprehensive school, but he had at last left it behind him.

He refused to be destroyed by guilt but he felt incredibly angry with himself. He had been duped by this stupid, contemptible girl. She had used him as a sperm-donor and benefit resource. For years ahead he would have to pay for the maintenance of a child conceived without his consent. This selfish, inadequate scrounger had exploited him and his family, and would now generate more beings in her own image. She would play the role of the pitiful victim, and leave him with a legacy which might affect him for the rest of his life. He did not deserve this fate, but the absurd and hypocritical society in which he lived would condemn only him. His decision was made. It was no good turning to the courts for sympathy or assistance. 'The circumstances of conception are irrelevant,' they would say. He drew strength from his own supportive family and friends, and from the example of his long-dead grandfather, to whom he had been very close.

As a young man during the war, his grandad had found himself in very similar circumstances, from which the war and his own courage had rescued him. He had paid the legal requirement in terms of maintenance for the child, but that was all. He had rescued himself from a loveless marriage and found true, lifelong love with another, who understood what he had endured before meeting her. With this wonderful relationship his former nightmare disappeared into the past. He had judged his situation for himself and acted; he had confidently listened to his own heart saying 'get out!'

Layla tried every method of emotional blackmail, persuasion and vindictiveness, but without success. She didn't need his money, she had plenty and the child had all the toys in the world. But one illusion had been peeled away. The pregnancy which she had been planning for years had failed in its purpose; she could not believe that her trump card had not succeeded. Now, she would have to go to all the trouble of finding someone else to impregnate her and offer marriage. In the meantime though, her little boy ensured that she had a comfortable two-bedroomed house plus benefits, and her occasional job was cash-in-hand. There were plenty of relatives conveniently close at hand for child-minding, and they supported her in not paying any taxes. Even going to 'uni' to pursue her then boyfriend had been free. When her deception had come to the attention of Social Services, she simply broke down in tears saying that all she had wanted to do was make her 'dead dad proud'. She had got away with this, and sub-letting her accommodation whilst away at university. The authorities preferred to concentrate on soft-targets rather than bother to pursue awkward debts.

Layla gloated over all the state support which she now received, plus the money from that 'snobby' past boyfriend. If nothing else, it was a way of getting back at his mother who obviously had no interest in her alleged grandchild. Anyway, it's her loss, thought Layla smugly. It did not occur to her that for some people genes alone mean nothing.

The young woman never learned from her experiences; she seemed incapable of mental or emotional development. When her boyfriend had been in the process of trying to end their relationship, she had simply ignored him and pleaded poor health. His honesty and integrity were either ignored or acted as a spur to become pregnant as quickly as possible. When he told her that they had no future together, that he neither wanted to live with her nor ever have children, she reacted with deceit and manipulation. Believing that she had only months to live, and taking his own finals within weeks, he responded to her with great patience.

Little did he realise that whilst he was ministering to her instead of studying, she had been visiting websites giving information on how to maximise her chances of pregnancy. Her motive was to create what she thought would be a permanent link with him and his family, and if that failed, there was always the Child Support Agency to harass him with. It would be his future finances under the spotlight, not hers. That was how the law worked. She could look forward to a new car from her uncle and the most expensive pram for the golden baby. Her boyfriend's parents lived in an expensive village; they might be another potential resource.

Several years later, there were changes afoot. Layla had a dark, tattooed fiancée and a new baby boy. His first outing had been to his grandfather's grave in the nearby cemetery. She was still hoping for the long-awaited golden girl. There had also been a change of government. The New-Labour fantasy had been overturned, to be replaced by David Cameron's coalition. One of their election promises was to reform the benefits system in favour of the tax-payer. During this debate there were many letters to the broadsheets on this topic, which could, at long last, be openly discussed. Layla and her family were either indifferent or unaware; they only read the tabloids and waited for the return of a Labour government. In the meantime, they uttered with outrage their constant, mindless refrain: 'It's disgusting.'

Letter to an unknown ...

Sir,

As the great writer Carlo Levi knew, the state is rarely a force for good. He was exiled to Southern Italy in the 1930s for anti-fascist activities.

Your Friday edition of *The Independent* included a large, threatening advertisement by the Child Support Agency. Why was this blatant piece of government propaganda, Orwellian in its prominence and aggressive message, displayed in your newspaper? Are you endorsing it?

The CSA presents itself as a responsible, beneficent organisation helping the innocent victims of those who are refusing to pay child maintenance. The CSA arrogantly and glibly claims to be acting in the best interests of the child; in almost all cases, this means targeting what the CSA sees as absconding, irresponsible fathers. This simplistic approach, which completely ignores the details of each individual case, typifies the current demonisation of men.

Thus the CSA is often the chief accomplice and unquestioning supporter of those who opt for voluntary single motherhood at the expense of both the state and those men who have been tricked into unwanted paternity. The law makes no distinction between genuine cases of paternal financial evasion or indifference after divorce, or separation of a couple, and those circumstances in which fathers are forced to provide money either for children with whom they have no contact, or those conceived without their consent.

Women are always seen as the victims in this struggle; all power resides with them. It is the woman who uses the CSA to initiate a review of the man's finances even though he may be unwilling or unable to pay.

Many members of the medical and legal profession have spoken of their private opposition to the way the CSA functions. It is frequently an outrageous instrument of state extortion. Because of the intervention of the CSA 'the circumstances of the conception of the child are unfortunately not relevant,' said one London solicitor. It is not right that child maintenance is assessed purely on a DNA paternity test. Men must be given the opportunity to explain why they are refusing to pay child support. It is because they have rightly rejected deceitfully imposed 'fatherhood', feeling only anger and estrangement. Women who have used men as paying 'sperm-donors', or whose motives include entrapment or revenge should not be encouraged by the CSA to seek yet another extension to the benefit support.

Women now have access to total contraceptive protection, and must take responsibility for this. They should also take the consequences when they use a deliberate pregnancy to test a relationship. Having lied about being on the pill and contrived to become pregnant, the woman puts pressure on the man and hopes to make him feel guilt-ridden. If the desired outcome of entrapment fails to succeed, then a late termination is still an option.

The time has come for somebody to protect the rights of men and listen to *their* version of events. A thorough, open debate on all this is absolutely essential, as is the urgent development of the male pill. Men should be *under the spotlight* in a positive way.

The N_2F_4 Collection: July 1978 – A Warning to the Chemist

Moon

On a beautiful early morning at the height of summer, the post-doctoral research fellow set out from Cambridge on his mission to Queen Mary College, London. In his blue plastic shopping bag he carried a 5-litre spherical vacuum flask with a ground-glass tap. This globe-like object was protectively wrapped in an old beige woolly, brought from home. It was important to have a covering layer to prevent any flying glass, should the flask implode during the return train journey with the gas.

The collection of the dinitrogen tetrafluoride had been arranged by the young researcher's supervising Professor, later to become head of the entire chemistry department at the University of Cambridge. This eminent academic had been a child protégée, having taken his 'A' levels at grammar school at the age of 12, but his emotional development had obviously lagged behind that of his intellect. Even in late middle-age he remained immature with a dysfunctional personality. He always rode to work on a small-wheeled ladies' bicycle, which belonged to his wife. Unofficially, he laid claim to a particular parking spot for his cycle; when, on one occasion, his place had been taken by another cyclist, he fell into a rage, repeatedly kicking the occupant's bike. This undignified tantrum was observed by all those in a departmental workshop situated on the top floor of the chemistry building and overlooking the car park. His childish behaviour and occasional lack of self-control was forgiven because of his scientific brilliance. In some ways his kind and motherly wife, a Canadian, had three offspring to care for. Batty, so called after his initials, was her precocious third child.

For the past year, his research team had included the man given the task of collecting the N_2F_4 from London. This post-doctoral assistant had completed his PhD at the University of Leeds, under the guidance of one of the Professor's former researchers who had left Cambridge to take up a lectureship at Leeds. He would never forget those three intensive years of conducting endless experiments in a small laboratory which was freezing in winter and roasting in summer. His supervisor, Dr Ian Campbell was an ultra-thrifty, slave driving Scotsman. The apparatus itself had to be built from scratch; it was fragile and temperamental. He was constantly having to test for pin-holes in the glass vacuum line. It took ages to close down in the evening after yet another day of experimental runs, which had to be in blackout conditions. As the cramped laboratory was windowless and relied solely on electric lighting, it was necessary to lock the door and switch off all the lights. No-one could enter or leave until the experiment was concluded. On countless days he was isolated in either a freezing or sweltering dark laboratory for more than eight hours at a time. On occasions he had to pee in a Dewar flask to avoid disturbance to the vital experiment. At the conclusion of each day Dr Campbell would come into the laboratory asking for the 'results'. He described himself to his several researchers as 'a measurer of rate constants', and was always irritated by what he perceived as their irreverent attitudes. His post-doctoral fellow used to wear shorts and a vest in the summer because of the unbelievable heat in his airless laboratory, where he toiled in the dark. Dr Campbell disapproved of this casual wear; he himself always wore a shirt, tie and sports-jacket, irrespective of temperatures. Another of his research students was addicted to cricket, which took precedence over chemistry during the summer and was also absorbed in the very long novel *War and Peace*. Ian Campbell regarded literary works as a waste of time, 'Anyone can loaf about on a sofa reading novels' he said. Jack tried to read Tolstoy during the occasional interludes between experimental runs, but Dr Campbell was always trying to catch him out. Jack and his fellow researcher, who was catching up with the daily newspapers had devised an elaborate warning system for the approach of the humourless and relentless Dr Campbell! The 'measurer of rate constants' never let up on his pressured students, but he himself had an ordered and relaxed routine. He never arrived early and always left for home by five o' clock; at least his predictability made him easy to deceive!

The Cambridge Professor felt sure that the young man would give good service as he had been very well trained at Leeds, in a highly-disciplined and respected faculty. However, a 12-month delay in getting a wall knocked down, for the building and installation of their infrared laser magnetic-resonance spectrometer and new tunable diode laser, had led to great frustration. Now that the apparatus was at last up and running, it was imperative to put it through its paces. A sense of urgency prevailed.

Dinitrogen tetrafluoride was needed because its thermal decomposition produced the NF_2 radical, which was known to absorb in the infrared region, and thus be observed with their spectrometer. If seen, they would then know that all was working well. The difficulty lay in finding a supplier for the gas, as BOC had stopped making it due to lack of demand. It seemed that at present it was only of academic use.

Fortunately for the cunning Professor, he had many former contacts to serve his purpose. He knew that an old ex-student, now at Queen Mary College, had some dinitrogen tetrafluoride which he was using in his current research group. As there was no academic rivalry or overlap in fields of research, the Professor's contact was happy to provide him with the gas.

The men arranged a time, and as, coincidentally, there was a laser exhibition on in Brighton during this period, it was agreed that they 'could kill two birds with one stone'. The Professor's research assistant would collect the gas and go to the exhibition in Brighton; both actions might be accomplished on the same day.

As the young post-doctoral fellow walked briskly along Lensfield Road, beneath the line of shady trees, he felt a sense of relief and excitement. He was longing to get his hands on this elusive gas and proceed with the long-awaited test runs and experiments. The entire team were awaiting results, especially as there were disquieting rumours of Japanese progress in this area of research.

The source of this gas was free, thanks to his Professor's pre-eminence in this field and the adulation of former colleagues, many of whom he had helped to achieve permanent positions at top universities. The confident research fellow looked forward to carrying out the experiments which would demonstrate that the apparatus would work properly; all he needed to do was look at a free radical for which the parameters were known.

During this easy-going era of the 1970s, long before Health and Safety were obsessed by risk, it was possible to feel perfectly relaxed about an entirely amateur manner of collecting a highly hazardous substance. The researcher's only concern was academic; he just wanted to get the N_2F_4 back to Cambridge without its escaping into the atmosphere. If he lost it because the flask imploded, he would have to return to Queen Mary College for some more, thus delaying the onset of experimental work. He did not want to lose the gas and fail in his scientific mission. He felt absolutely no concern for his personal safety; if an accident occurred then the only adverse consequences would be for science.

He sat down in the railway carriage, with the blue plastic shopping-bag held firmly between his knees. Luckily, the train was almost empty so there had been no pushing and shoving. When he returned later that night it would still be warm and daylight would streak the sky. There had been no special instructions from the Professor, and nothing had been discussed. He knew exactly what to do and looked forward to being by the sea in Brighton. The greatest risks to life at this time, he mused, came from Irish terrorism and Sinclair's C5 'buggy' on the congested roads of Cambridge. Several times he had been forced to mount the pavement by these ridiculous vehicles; they did not combine well with fast-moving cyclists weaving in and out of traffic. When they obstructed his path or he glimpsed their stupid little flag-topped masts vibrating at eye-level, when his head was down low over the handlebars of his racing bike, he frequently made a rude 'V' sign at them. They were driven by rich, pompous adults who behaved worse than small children in pedal go-carts. Cambridge was a dangerous place to travel slowly.

Fortunately, it was easy to escape from the vehicle-laden streets of the busy city. There were so many quiet and serene places like the wonderful botanical gardens, where the scientist now on the train to London often found his depressed fellow research assistant sitting alone on a bench. Not that you had to leave the chemistry department to find tranquillity and solitude; the basement laboratories had been sardonically referred to as 'the area where the lights were always out'. In theory, they were a hive of intense academic activity, but it was sometimes difficult to substantiate this popular image. Many of the postgraduate students were simply inept and relied on the unspoken Cambridge system of 'collaborative' PhDs to gain their final qualification. Furthermore, many of the older professors persisted in their favouritism towards Cambridge graduates. Thus, there were a disproportionate number of PhDs with mediocre first-degree results who nevertheless gained research studentships. A Catholic mafia also operated within the department so that, as long as you were Catholic and a graduate of Cambridge, you were almost certain to be admitted to a PhD. If you were then discovered to be sub-standard you could still rely on the 'collaborative' system to help in gaining your research degree. When the time came to seek employment, this favouritism towards the 'home-grown' product operated again. Job vacancies from top scientific institutions, which traditionally employed Cambridge people, were sent to the professors in Lensfield Road and they would then recommend a candidate. Thus, one of their own graduates would fill the post. The young researcher collecting his flask of gas from Queen Mary College on behalf of his Professor, remembered him saying: 'You know what you're getting, when you get a Cambridge man.' This unabashed preference for graduates of Cambridge was the subject of many ironic jokes from the small number of postgraduates and postdoctoral fellows from other universities, including those in America who were a breath of fresh air.

The unstuffy American approach to cricket was both relished and condemned. As baseball and cricket share a common heritage and the former also has its roots in 18th century England, it is not surprising that the Americans in the departmental team soon adapted and adjusted their style to encompass traditional English cricket. One player in particular, named David Jaffa, saw no estrangement between the two team games with a personal duel at their heart. He combined a batsman's grip with a swinging baseball posture and smashed the balls to the boundary.

One fine summer's day friends took David to Audley End Mansion to see a traditional English cricket match on the beautiful lawns in front of the great house – he was bewitched and loved wearing whites, even though on the very first occasion of wearing them he wore long socks and pulled them up over his white trousers! Subsequently, he fell in love with the game, especially its rituals and traditional clothes. He was immensely proud to have mastered cricket and play for the Chemistry Department at Cambridge. In fact he became the most exiting, talented and committed batsman in the side.

The Americans were very popular with the other temporary members of the chemistry department. They had come to Cambridge because of its outstanding history and reputation; it still retained tremendous kudos. But once they had spent a term in the basement of Lensfield Road, they started to question their assumptions. Many of them found the facilities impoverished and primitive in the extreme; they were not surprised that after almost 2 years, the University was still searching for a top academic to replace Professor Norrish, who had retired as Head of Chemistry. A famous American academic had declined the offer, presumably because of the paltry salary and lack of research funding. Cambridge expected the very, very best when they took someone from outside, but they could no longer take it for granted that Cambridge was seen as a Mecca for the world's most brilliant minds. The temporary acting Head of Chemistry was becoming an embarrassment as he was in mental decline. After a brief and disastrous appointment, the Committee eventually and of necessity decided to appoint a Cambridge man. This Professor was undoubtedly the most suitably qualified for the job and should have been offered it in the first place. Venomous academic in-fighting must have been the explanation for why he was not originally chosen. Anyway, after so many years of waiting, he finally had his revenge on some of his short-sighted colleagues.

But by the time this event occurred, the post-doctoral fellow sent to London for the free supply of N_2F_4 had left Cambridge University, having been there for five years. He had never had a good relationship with his Professor as he was too independent in attitude. When he published his research, and he published a great many papers, he did not expect to be subservient to his Professor. The great man thought otherwise, knowing that without his name, prestige, and brilliance, there would have been no research funding in the first place.

Neither did this particular research assistant attend the Professor's numerous 'at home' social occasions. One was supposed to dress up, make polite conversation, admire the polished-stone collection at the entrance, and then enjoy the remainder of the evening wine-tasting. Polished stones were the hobby of his wife, and the lovely wines were his passion. As Master of Emmanuel College, he had limitless access to the wine collection there. He was very snobbish about such matters, as he was about having to mix with plebeians like the non-academic staff. In the old days at Cambridge there was simply no question of the departmental photograph, exhibited on the staircase, including any technicians. Clear distinctions were made and maintained between intellectuals and the 'others'. Like the college servants, they were privileged to be of use to their masters, but must never be treated as equals. They were horribly underpaid but that could not be helped; it was just part of the correct order of things.

However, despite his resistance to change, the philistines were gaining ground and the precious hierarchy was tumbling down around him. Even in the departmental canteen he still ate at a separate table, (even though he himself always drank the dregs of his tea from a saucer), where he was joined solely by fellow academics, but the technicians and clerical staff were moving ever closer. A further indignity was that he now had to play cricket with them at the departmental Sports Day. He adored his cricket and the superb teas that were laid on by the College caterers. The food at Cambridge was lavish and glorious beyond belief, and there was nothing lovelier than playing cricket at King's or Churchill. On their part, the despised technicians got stuck into the wonderful summer spread of delicacies, always concluded with strawberries and cream, and ignored most of the senior academics. One of the glassblowing technicians, who was a talented amateur cricketer, joked that it would be the end of his job if he bowled out the Prof! There was very little mutual respect between these different social groups, and the Cambridge underclass was becoming increasingly resentful.

They thoroughly enjoyed Batty's discomfiture when his son and daughter, especially the latter, embarrassed him at a cricket match at King's. Just as her father was padding up, ready to go in to bat, the convent educated daughter said loudly 'daddy, what's a "box", what is it for?' Reddening and mumbling her professor father said that he would explain later, but she persisted in raising her voice and shouting the question over and over again until he at last gave a detailed explanation! On the same occasion his son was repeatedly reprimanded for eating too many chocolate bars, cakes and helpings of dessert; he was a large boy and a bit of a glutton. However, as the brilliant 'Batty' was so childlike himself he was not altogether comfortable in the parental role, especially when admonishing his children. The humble technical staff could hardly be blamed for the occasional laugh at his expense.

Some of this irreverence had spilled over to the postgraduate students, and even a few of the post-docs. As he approached Kings Cross Station, and held on tightly to the handles of the blue plastic bag, the young researcher smiled to himself as he remembered an especially funny example of insubordination by a drunken technician and postdoctoral fellow. The two of them had been out drinking at lunchtime; they were both attempting to drown miseries and problems in their personal lives. The postdoc had drawn down the blackout curtains of his laboratory, thereby giving the impression that he was engaged in experimental work and must not be disturbed. In reality, he was enjoying a heavy drinking session with his technician friend. The apparatus included a large metal box with sliding doors, which contained a spectrometer. He referred to this as his 'cocktail cabinet' and when he slid open the doors an array of bottles was revealed. The two friends continued to drink and invited others from the department to join them. The laughter grew louder until suddenly there was a heavy knock on the curtained door-window. Inside the small laboratory there was silence, but within moments the door opened to reveal the great Professor who was showing his department to a visiting academic. As he entered the room, the now-nervous technician fell against a huge glass vac line and knocked it over, smashing it to pieces. In trying to recover an upright position he crashed around, clumsily breaking even more equipment. The Professor was scarlet with fury, and uttered the words 'please continue'. The door closed and then almost immediately re-opened. 'I meant, discontinue,' stammered the seething Professor and slammed the door behind him. Everyone in the laboratory sobered up amidst the broken glass, beer bottles and general devastation. The technician hastily returned to his work. Much as he resented his lowly status he was well aware that in other universities the staff and students would have built their own apparatus. They would have been sent on glass-blowing courses and to learn other rudimentary skills; technical backup would not have been needed. The postdoc knew full well that he would either be dismissed from the University, or receive a huge dressing-down. The Professor liked to win, whether it was in the crease or doing battle with his inferiors.

The Professor's postdoctoral research assistant continued on his errand. Having arrived at Kings Cross mainline station, he now took the Metropolitan line to Aldgate. Luckily, the underground was not too busy so he sat tranquilly with his precious fragile flask squeezed between his knees. Alighting at Aldgate, he climbed the stairs and exited into the bright sunlight of Whitechapel Road. He had quite a long walk ahead of him, all the way up Whitechapel Road, past the large Jewish cemetery, then continuing along Mile End Road to Queen Mary College. He would have plenty of time to vacuum the flask down on their vac line, in order to extract all the air, and leave this in process while he went to the laser exhibition in Brighton. It would be coffee-time when he reached the college, and they would be able to drive to Brighton straight after lunch in the old banger owned by a student of his Professor's former colleague. All the aims of this day-trip would be completed as economically as possible.

As the small group of scientific researchers drove through central London, the day became even hotter. It reminded them of the incredible summer of 1976 when the heatwave had lasted for months. Every morning from late May onwards, one awoke to clear blue sky and burning heat. The man from Leeds remembered his small rented cottage in Meanwood where, in that very year, he had heard of the tragic death of David Munrow, the early-music specialist. And later on in 1976, shortly before Christmas, the composer Benjamin Britten had died. In some ways his own Cambridge Professor resembled Britten who had been brilliant but childish. Neither could bear to be beaten at anything, were ruthless, and devoid of an adult sense of humour. Their accelerated intellectual development appeared to have arrested other areas of the normal human being. They also seemed alike in their willingness to be impressed by mediocrities, as long as they were wealthy ones. They were blinded by money and social class. He called to mind a notorious incident at Churchill College Sports Day, when a popular writer of unreadable trash, whose wife happened to work in the chemistry department and belonged to the College, had turned up at the sports ground with his publicity entourage in tow. A number of academics, including his Professor, were sycophantically fussing over this 'celebrity' author and his photographer. A few dissenting voices were openly mocking this embarrassing nonsense and refused to participate in such blatant egotism.

This break-away group clapped loudly when the ghastly wife of the popular author was quickly bowled-out by one of their colleagues. She had made a huge display of being the only woman in the cricket side, complete with tiny gym skirt and huge leg pads, and was furious when she was dismissed without scoring a single run. Out for a duck in a maiden over! The Professor was furious, and when his brief innings ended similarly at the hands of the same bowler, the said bowler wondered if his position at the University would soon be terminated.

Before this sense of malaise, insecurity and spitefulness had permeated the chemistry department it had been a domain of supreme achievement and eccentricity. Its former head, the famous Professor Norrish, was seemingly irreplaceable. Not only had he been a brilliant academic but also an alcoholic and martinet whose former students still told stories of his outlandish behaviour and often hilarious feats. There were fewer and fewer colourful characters left in academia, that wonderful side of university life was sadly in decline.

The researcher on his way to the laser exhibition in Brighton suddenly felt hungry and was glad that he had remembered to bring a banana. It was unlikely that there would be time for eating after the exhibition, and certainly no-one from Queen Mary College would have thought of providing food. His hunger brought to mind one of the great 'Norrish' stories, told by his former student DD.

When not in the laboratory or his favourite local pub, the Nobel-prize-winning Professor was often to be found in his office. On this occasion DD sat down opposite Norrish, who was seated at his desk. To the great surprise of his then-student, the Professor opened a drawer and took out a pie which he placed on the desk, saying, 'You see that Drysdale, that's my lunch. You have it.' Not wishing to cause offence to the great man, DD responded to this autocratic command by reluctantly eating the said pie!

Encounters in the Professor's office were fraught with such unpleasant surprises, but meeting him for lunch in *The Spread Eagle* pub was even more unwise. The legendary Professor had his very own corner chair, which he loved to use for impromtu lunchtime meetings which often extended into closing time. DD turned up promptly to discuss a problem in reaction kinetics, only to leave many hours later in a state of complete drunkenness. In contrast, Professor Norrish could consume large quantities of alcohol without any apparent ill effect or impairment of his intellectual faculties. DD remembered to avoid *The Spread Eagle* in the future!

Another oft-repeated story also centred around Professor Ronald George Wreyford Norrish, FRS. The research chemist now journeying to Brighton, had been given the anecdote by his PhD supervisor at Leeds University. It was yet another joyous account from the Cambridge glory days when there was no health and safety oppression. Professor Norrish had wanted to look at some spectral lines from the moon to see if there were any gases present. It was necessary to observe the reflection of moonlight and search for spectral lines emanating from this light. The experiment required taking a large spectrometer out onto Parker's Piece at night. This large, grassy, public area provided the requisite space under a full moon. The spectrometer was loaded onto a four-wheeled trolley with a handle, rather like a railway porter's conveyance. As the research team trundled the trolley along Lensfield Road, past the famous Scott-Polar Research Institute, and onwards to Parker's Piece, they were abruptly halted by a policeman. He asked them what they were doing, and when they replied that they were taking a spectrum of the moon, he booked them for being in possession of a vehicle without brakes or lights! The research group had to abandon the project and return back to the department. Fortunately, Professor Norrish found the events of the night highly amusing. Perhaps it was another example of Midsummer Madness, worthy of Shakespeare's rustics!

By the end of the hot afternoon in Brighton, it was time to return to Queen Mary College and collect the N_2F_4. Refreshed by sea-breezes, regency elegance, and the forces of nature, the young chemist felt happy to be homeward bound. He reflected on the death of the remarkable Professor Norrish in the previous month. Ronald Norrish had been appointed to the Chair of Physical Chemistry in 1937, and had remained as head of department until 1965 when he retired as Emeritus Professor of Physical Chemistry in the University. He always maintained his presence in the department and in many ways he was irreplaceable. His death on June 7, 1978 had marked the end of a truly amazing era. He would never have allowed a popular novelist, compulsive liar and fantasist, to be invited to play cricket at the University as a 'celebrity' guest of the chemistry team.

Norrish, however, adhered to old style thinking on class and hierarchy. His last research student was David Husain, who had graduated with a first-class honours degree from Manchester University when, arguably, it had the finest department of chemistry in the world. Nevertheless, when David in 1959 began his PhD work under R G W Norrish, the professor said jokingly that he should really repeat his BSc as it was not from Cambridge.

David Hussain quickly ascended the academic ladder at the University to become a Reader, and Fellow of Pembroke College, but did not endorse the Norrish and Batty attitude of segregation between academics and non-academic members of staff. His kindliness and consideration for others extended to everybody irrespective of their position. His idol was Bismarck, but his 2007 obituary by Professor John Meurig Thomas, ('John Thomas is a prick' said the graffiti written on the ladies toilet door in the chemistry department) quotes from one of Jane Austen's letters to embody Husain's qualities as a human being: 'Incline us, O God, to think humbly of ourselves, to be severe only in the examination of our own conduct, to consider our fellow creatures with kindness'.

Unusually for a Cambridge academic David Husain was without self-importance, malice or rancour, or so it seemed to his fellow dons. His mixed Muslim Indian and Russian Jewish background probably contributed to his generosity of spirit. However, his brief and disastrous marriage seemed to vindicate Batty's theory of separation by intellect. David was more English than the English and for the technicians he was a figure of fun, especially when he fell victim to the matchmaking skills of a departmental secretary.

This ambitious lady snared him for her daughter, but the marriage was over in weeks. David was somewhat of a valetudinarian and used to shuffle around the chemistry department like someone three times his age. It took him about five minutes to cross Lensfield Road because he was so slow and hesitant, and he always wrapped himself up in large heavy overcoats, even in mid-summer. When he made the decision to marry he probably thought that his wife would mother him and relieve him of any domestic responsibilities. According to the perceptive technicians, David 'Insane' as they called him 'had failed in marriage because he was unfamiliar with the use of a tea-towel'. He was accustomed to being waited on and became neurotic if challenged. Members of the chemistry department noted that he was phobic about using the photocopier; if anyone was behind him in the queue he became deeply agitated and flustered. After his catastrophic experiment with marriage he withdrew to a cloistered but safe existence in Pembroke College. The technician's disrespectful verdict was that like Batty, he didn't have 'a decent f... in him!' In befriending 'the common man' David Husain was under an illusion in thinking that the respect and goodwill was reciprocated. And in his later years Dr Husain revealed the latent snobbery which, according to the technical staff had only been artfully concealed. In conversation with a technician about his recent holiday in the English Lake District, he said disparagingly 'What *sort* of people go to the Lake district?'

The postdoctoral researcher collected his flask of dinitrogen tetrafluoride and wrapped it carefully in the old beige woolly, lest it should implode during the return journey. Once again he picked up the old blue plastic shopping bag and made his way along Whitechapel Road, past the Jewish cemetery and onwards to the tube station. In the roar of traffic and the dusty London heat he recalled a cricket match at the King's/Selwyn ground at Cambridge; the two colleges shared the facility. On this occasion he had been fielding near the boundary and pavilion; the infamous novelist, soon to become a member of the House of Lords and later an inmate of HM prison service, was fielding on the same side. In the crease and facing the bowler was the current, short-lived, Welsh Head of the Chemistry Department. When he had accepted the professorship at Cambridge, he had brought along most of his own research group from his former university in Wales. One of his postdoctoral fellows was batting at the other end, and they were talking to each other in Welsh. 'God,' said the crime novelist and imposter, 'They sound like a load of bloody pakis.' This appalling but typical comment was directed at all those within earshot, including the young researcher and a laboratory technician.

Remembering those now far-away days in the 1970s, especially his lone mission to obtain N_2F_4, the no-longer-young research chemist felt a mixture of nostalgia, amusement and relief. In many ways he had been glad to say goodbye to the chemistry department at Cambridge and make a highly successful career in the nuclear industry. Some of his fellow researchers in the late 1970s had been less fortunate. Disillusioned by his long postdoctoral years at Cambridge, where he had spent most of his time installing a complex vibration-free floor, rather than doing top-level science, one contemporary had finished up as a tax inspector. As far as the Professor was concerned, he had served his purpose in research, and had better get himself a job outside academia, before it was too late. Naturally, he wished him well, but his future was no concern of his. This was an austere era with few new permanent posts becoming available in university. It was very dangerous for future employment prospects in the outside world, to become an eternal post-doc. The grand title belied the humble status. Industry might treat such a person with contempt; far too many of his students fantasised about future academic positions. They hung on at Cambridge for far too long, only to have their hopes dashed and then find it difficult to fit in anywhere else.

At least this had not been the unenviable fate of the Professor's 1978 postdoctoral researcher, sent to London for a flask of dinitrogen tetrafluoride. And health and safety regulations were now an integral part of his work in nuclear research. The charming and lax indifference to safety by the universities of the 1970s now seemed unthinkable – sourcing and acquiring a small amount of N_2F_4 in 2010 would be a very different problem for an academic. Nowadays there were safety-data sheets and toxicity studies published by TOXNET.

The toxicity classification for dinitrogen tetrafluoride was HIGHLY HAZARDOUS. Its decomposition products are hydrogen fluoride and nitrogen oxides. Because N_2F_4 is a strong fluorinating agent towards many substances, it is extremely toxic. The most intriguing property of this gas, which was discovered in 1957, is an ability to dissociate at room temperature and above, to give the free radical NF_2. Dissociation is its really important characteristic; this is why the Professor of Chemistry insisted on acquiring some for his groundbreaking experiments in the summer of 1978. With the undergraduates having gone down for the long vacation there was more time to concentrate on research, and less teaching to attend to. Sadly, the City remained congested because it was full of Japanese tourists. Many local people wore silly badges saying 'I'm not a tourist. I live here'; Cambridge was at its best in the autumn when the mist hovered on the river and all the trees in the exquisite college gardens looked glorious. The atmosphere was unique, and Kings College Chapel, the most beautiful chapel in the world, looked sublime amidst the softened outlines.

The transportation of N_2F_4 in the year 2010 would have required the use of a stainless steel cylinder. Safety glass and protective gloves would have been worn at all times. If inhaled, the gas could cause very nasty respiratory problems; there had been extensive toxicity studies on rats, mice, and guinea pigs. Inhalation by the rat had caused difficulties in the lungs and thorax; in the mouse sense organs had been damaged and convulsions were also observed.

The continuing presence of Stephen Hawking as Lucasian Professor of Theoretical Physics, a chair once occupied by Sir Isaac Newton, gave Cambridge University some glamour, but so many memorable characters had now retired or died. At the time of the amateurish and risky N_2F_4 expedition, there had been a delightful, fun-loving member of the academic staff who served a tennis ball by using an arm action which resembled a windmill, and could dance all evening with a full glass of red wine balancing in his pocket. Rivalry and pressure surrounded him and had given rise to a couple of nervous breakdowns, but his humanity and humour had remained intact. Staring into the abyss had enriched him as a person.

He was almost the only member of the academic staff to laugh at the rude balloons and music chosen by post-graduates and post-doctoral fellows for a 1970s departmental party. A technician D.J. had been set up to play tracks by Ian Dury and the Blockheads, including the comic song *There ain't half been some clever bastards*. The lyrics included hilarious references to iconic scientists, including Einstein, expressed in very witty but crude and irreverent words. As a breast and phallus balloon floated across Batty's face, he wafted it away in irritation and at last noticed the satirical words of the song about doing some 'splitiness' and frightening everybody 'shitless'! Batty's research team had done it as a joke, but he was not amused. He pulled a face of horrified disapproval and ordered Alfie, the technician, to turn it off at once. He noted all those who were clearly enjoying this lewdness and vented his temper upon them, including the popular drunken colleague dancing with a wine glass.

Perhaps the very best thing about university during that time was that it nurtured and protected brilliant, singular, individuals who would have been misfits in any other context. And associated institutions retained their bewitching treasures; artistic immortality resided in the colleges and museums. Even on a day-trip to Cambridge in the summer of 2010, it is possible to visit the Fitzwilliam Museum in which resides their *Head of Antinous* ... Beloved and God.

The Brontë Brothers of Cheshire

Vampire bat

Her three sons were named after Peter Pan and his lost boys. Unfortunately, the longed-for daughter had never arrived; she was, of course, to have been called 'Wendy'. As the 'little mother', the firstborn girl did not materialise; the three boys had only their parents to anchor them at home. From her earliest maternal experience she had been afraid that the boys would one day fly from their safe nest in rural Cheshire. Although ambitious for them in the wider world, she simply could not bear the thought of being left; she would be lost without them. Hopefully, they would forever remain in childhood.

As the boys inevitably grew, matured, and passed through puberty, they were overtaken by sexual urges which seemed to be divisive, and drive them from home. During this period of semi-estrangement from their parents and each other, no-one would have guessed that years later they would re-unite through the written word. As young adults their parents seemed to lose them to autism, crime, and madness. Even 'Wendy' could not have held them together in their desperate urge to escape.

The firstborn son had been anti-social from a very early age. He suffered from unpredictable outbursts of rage and violence which were very difficult to control; he soon became unpopular with other parents. He felt safe and calm only when confined to his room with his hi-tech toys and computer. He ceased to join the family for meals, preferring to eat alone from his lap-tray, facing his bedroom wall. Unseen and unseeing, he felt relaxed enough to eat and drink. But how was he to satisfy his sexual fantasies from an internet connection? His parents were ultra-conventional, and deeply unsympathetic to what they termed 'unsuitable outside influences'. They disapproved of outsiders, or anyone who might be on the social or economic fringes of society. Scientific, clever, and industrious, the father set a stolid example which he expected all his sons to follow. There was no room for rebellion, and no time to waste on things like hip-hop or rappers. Friends with unusual nicknames like 'Noz' were scrutinised with hostility and suspicion.

As the eldest son grew up into a disappointment, attention focussed on the always-problematic middle child. Disillusioned by the comprehensive system and its seemingly negative effect on their first son, the parents decided to educate boy number two in the private sector. As he was very bright he found it easy to win a scholarship to a high-performing, single-sex, former grammar school now operating a rigorous selection procedure.

However, despite this disciplined, academic environment, the second son appeared to be following his brother in all the wrong directions. Wayward and un-cooperative his interest in science decreased whilst his curiosity about sexual experimentation was on the increase.

Disastrously, his big brother had made a secret dash to an assignation down South. Having arranged the sexual encounter on the internet, the interchange was a disaster and he returned home to Cheshire with his 'tail between his legs'. Humiliated and traumatised, he confessed all to his parents and resumed his days on the computer keyboard. His parents decided that he needed careful watching and control.

Disconcertingly, second son seemed to have the same base inclinations. Whenever he left the house his parents wondered what he was up to; they trusted neither him nor any of his friends. Further attempts were made to confine him with his school texts, but he found cunning excuses to escape from home. School clubs for activities such as chess provided excellent cover for a drinking session with friends.

His progress towards GCSEs was steady, and occasionally inspired, but there were increasing episodes of rude, anti-social behaviour at the houses of parental friends. This came to a climax in the summer vacation before the start of A-levels. Having been invited to a post-exam party, he quickly became drunk on vodka and ran wild, digging up the garden, and destroying trees and ornaments. When the adults returned, they found that the son of their long-term close friends had done untold damage to their home and garden. Not only did he admit to his delinquent behaviour, but he showed absolutely no remorse.

The next thunderbolt came when his elite school refused to admit him to their sixth-form. Despite excellent exam results, they were disturbed by his attitudes to authority and the school ethos. He would simply have to leave and become someone else's problem.

Middle boy showed no regret at leaving his school; he felt no attachment to the place. If his dismissal was a shock then he certainly did not reveal this. He was perfectly happy to be admitted to an outstanding sixth-form college, one of the best in the country. As it was quite a long daily journey to the college, he thought that he might learn to drive as soon as he reached his seventeenth birthday. His parents were enthusiastic about this as his father was fed up with acting as a taxi service.

After many lessons with his frustrated and exasperated father, it was clear that second son had problems. Just as he never looked left and right when crossing the road, so he looked neither left nor right when driving a car. His father soon realised that his middle boy was impervious to other road users and pedestrians. The horror and danger of this shocked him profoundly; he realised that for years he had been in denial. The boy's perceptive best friend had always humorously commented on this lack of spatial awareness, but the ambitious father had not been listening. In general, he was dismissive of others; he arrogantly assumed that his sons were flawless. This patronising attitude and blindness to his son's obvious danger zones irritated the one true friend but he let it pass without comment. The entire family appeared to be unaware that they were all affected by personality disorders. The bemused and patient friend endured and remained loyal to middle boy. His experiences with this dysfunctional family and another dyspraxic friend were a good foundation for his later career as an English teacher in a school for children with special needs. His older sister had always joked that some of her own friends, during the awkward teenage years, had been the perfect preparation for her future as a mental-health social worker.

It was obvious to the non-judgemental one true friend that the three brothers all exhibited core symptoms of autism. When he first met middle boy at sixth-form college, he had excellent verbal communication skills, but was uneasy with eye-to-eye contact and manifested very awkward body posture. Also, his conversations tended to take the form of monologues; in order to maintain dialogue he had to be prompted. He seemed incapable of empathising with others and remained detached from the joy, or sorrow of his family and college friends. On one occasion, he had been intercepted when trying to kill his 'irritating' little brother; he showed no remorse for his action. This indifference to rules and obligations infuriated his teachers; they labelled him as rude, arrogant and impervious to criticism. He came across as a very unsympathetic character; a young man who mistakenly believed that he was the centre of the universe. The antagonism of his teachers towards him increased.

There is no doubt that he could be a most unrewarding friend. He borrowed money without seeing the need to pay it back, and failed to turn up for the twenty-first birthday celebrations of his one true friend. His excuse was that he just 'couldn't be bothered to get out of bed', because he had stayed up all night during the previous week.

This ingratitude was all the more deplorable when bearing in mind second son's college days, and his dependency on the unwavering support of his friend. Every Wednesday afternoon when the sixth-form college closed to allow for sporting activities or private study, middle boy would go to the home of his one true friend, and after a lunch of cheese on toast, they would compose and record their very clever rap songs until called for an evening meal by the friend's mother. Second son benefited from and enjoyed the kindness of this family; his own father was hostile to 'rap'. He later blamed it for influencing his middle son's decline into fantasy and criminality. As far as he was concerned, 'rapping' and drugs were synonymous. On those rare occasions when he understood the lyrics, he was horrified! In his opinion, rappers represented the current trend to subvert all civilised values.

Failure to engage fully with the college lecturers cost second son his first-choice university, but he plodded off happily enough to a disastrous education course chosen for him by his parents. He rebelled by missing lectures and lying in bed. His diet was a pizza for breakfast, a pizza for lunch, and a pizza for the evening meal. He found this routine easy and cheap and enough to satisfy his very limited energy output. It also meant that he didn't even have to leave the house in Leeds.

Obviously, his regime could not last. In order to qualify as a primary-school teacher it was necessary to turn up for teaching practice. As he hated kids and the classroom atmosphere, it was obviously an impossible career choice. It had been imposed on him by his parents but he didn't really mind one way or the other. His father phoned every morning to check that he was in lectures, so he just turned off the phone and continued sleeping. He enjoyed the music scene in Leeds and the contacts made via the internet. It was worth getting out of bed to DJ or pursue 'milfs' – his latest addiction was to sexually-desperate, middle-aged women. There might even be money to be made in these shadowy areas.

When he was removed from the teaching course he was relieved and complacent that he would soon find something less boring. Luckily, he was taken into the English department and his father would finance his wasted year. Nothing was lost and he now had even longer to find his feet in the Leeds low-life.

His parents monitored him carefully, or so they thought. But, in reality, it was easy to elude their questions and pretend that he was rolling steadily towards a respectable career, in publishing perhaps. They only saw what they wanted to see; this had always been the case. Middle son laughed silently at his deluded father. 'Egotism stands in the way of moral enlargement,' wrote George Eliot in *Middlemarch*; she could have been describing his father, thought the second boy in the family from rural Cheshire. He smiled to himself and arranged to meet his sprawling date. His big brother had messed everything up on his very first attempt at meeting for sex. The frequently overlooked younger brother, situated between autism and genuine academic brilliance, could certainly overtake them all when it came to finding compliant women. Also, he was doing enough to get by at University, so had plenty of time for recreational pursuits.

It was obvious to any street-wise native of Leeds that a naïve character such as middle boy would eventually get into deep water. Flirting with drug-taking and dealers was ultimately a route to the police station and the courts. If you were a first offender from a privileged background then no excuses would be made. The law would make an example of you, and from a police perspective you were a soft target, good for their crime statistics.

His downfall came rapidly; he was unaware that he had been the target of a policewoman's 'sting'. During an operation in the city centre he had stupidly and unknowingly tried to sell an ecstasy tablet to an undercover policewoman. Some weeks later he was arrested and after many, many months finally sent to prison for two years.

The one true friend from college days was the only person who took the trouble to keep in touch and send letters. The inmate's replies were full of foolish bravado and exaggerated stories of toughness. The good friend was irritated but not deceived; perhaps it was necessary to develop such a shell amidst the boredom and indignity of life in jail. Boasting and bragging were probably an inevitable outcome, although it was especially tedious when communicated through the written word. The truth was that he had been outwitted and caught; it was a simple case of *hubris* and *nemesis*. There were no profound truths or philosophical debates to arise from the rather silly and sordid chain of events. And when second son emerged from confinement he would rely on the financial support and safe haven of the family home in prosperous Cheshire.

Having acquired a criminal record for his two-year custodial sentence, there would be a lengthy period of rehabilitation before he was able to seek mainstream employment. Although, technically, his conviction would be spent, under the Criminal Justice and Immigration Act 2008 which amended the Rehabilitation of Offenders Act 1974, any future employer would have access to details of his prior convictions, reprimands and cautions. Mainstream employment would remain a dream for his family; he himself did not wish to engage with the conventional skilled workplace. His only jobs to date had been factory work and strawberry-picking, which he had really enjoyed. He relished its simple repetitive nature and the company of his fellow workers, none of whom spoke English. Also, it felt good to be outside in wide open spaces feeling the hot sun beating down on his back. In the same way that he had strong food likes and dislikes such as eating dry Weetabix and avoiding mushrooms, he enjoyed unusual preoccupations. Fruit-picking gave him the mental freedom to fantasise about mature women looking for sex, porn and perversion. Living with his wide spectrum autistic siblings in Cheshire would not be such a grim fate after all. His sole true friend thought that collectively, the three boys resembled the mysterious, possibly autistic, ocean-covered planet in Stanislaw Lem's psychological sci-fi novel, *Solaris*.

Nevertheless, the prodigal son returned home defiant. He was determined to prove that his time 'away' had turned him into a writer with lucrative prospects ahead. He would use his documented conversations with hard-line prisoners to contribute to the mass-market 'true-crime' genre. Along with 'misery memoirs' this stuff was dominating the supermarket bookshelves!

This was not quite the career which his parents had envisaged for him, especially as they believed that they had kept him away from all 'bad' influences and malign companions, but his success would triumph over their prejudices. His older and younger brothers would envy him and perhaps seek to emulate his skills. Three former 'geeks' might, however improbably, become the 'Brontë brothers of Cheshire'! And the impetus behind this transformation would have come, appropriately, from Yorkshire.

After several months of very hard work and intense writing, the middle boy had his manuscript ready to dispatch to several publishers. He felt very hopeful of a positive response and excellent monetary outcome. Seated with his laptop in the comfort and privacy of home, he complacently endured the electronic ankle tag and the curfew it enforced. These minor nuisances and infringements of his liberty would soon pass whilst he was making positive use of his experiences in prison. And he rather enjoyed seeing his attractive young probation officer. She had told him that their meetings were a pleasure in comparison with her usual round of violent and aggressive former prisoners.

Second son resented the excessive editorial input, choice of pseudonym and title dictated by the mass-market publishing house, but as a first-time writer he had to agree to their terms and conditions. At least he was going to be given an advance, a rare thing in these hard-pressed times – so he could not complain. Obviously, there could be no book-signings as he must remain anonymous. Anyway, it would be great to see his paperback on the shelves, and hopefully selling well to the 'true-crime' addicts. He had to make the most of his limited material and niche area; it was no use expecting to write literary fiction. As an ex-prisoner with one published book, he could go on to write a sequel with his remaining stuff, and then become a ghost-writer for football-hooligan memoirs. It would be hard work but pay enough to tick over whilst living at home. Also, ghost-writing was good for him. As he had to relate to and understand others in finding their 'voice', it was a form of personal therapy.

His mother now had two of her lost boys at home, but what of the youngest? He had been the exception and gladdened the heart of his father by excelling at science, going on to do a PhD. He lived like a hermit at university, completely absorbed in his research to the exclusion of all else, until tragedy struck.

Towards the end of his postgraduate research he experienced a psychotic episode, probably brought on by extreme stress. He left the university saying that he would never return to the sciences. He was ill for a long time; middle boy described him as having 'gone mad', and not wanting to go back to 'being sane'. The mental illness had proved to be a route to creativity. 'Since going mad my little brother is much happier,' said second son indifferently. He too was now writing and had already had a short story published. The firstborn brother, having been made redundant from his computer-based job at home, had at first moped endlessly but was also now writing.

Just as physical activity is vital to mental health, so the medical profession has recently documented the health-related effects of creative and expressive writing. The Department of Clinical Psychology at the University of Hull has published studies of poetry and immune function, they report some of the first empirical biological evidence for the poetry–health link. The cognitive-behavioural bases of 'writing therapy' include the informative function of emotions, self-regulation, re-framing, and dealing more effectively with negative feelings. A unique project at the University of Liverpool uses literature to help people with depression: *Get Into Reading* is founded on the idea that great literature can improve your mental health; it is an exhortation to live.

It seemed that the three brothers, all with problems, but vastly improved, were actually happiest when at home writing. The lost boys of their mother's imagination were all safely in her care, no longer facing the difficulties of trying to live independently. Not one of them wished anymore to fly away – reclaimed, they would create and never age. Something peculiarly precious, beautiful and fleeting might be retained forever, without dissolving into the more assertive and aggressive tones of manhood.